go
girl

Brilliant
Besties

hardie grant EGMONT

Brilliant Besties
published in 2013 by
Hardie Grant Egmont
Ground Floor, Building 1, 658 Church Street
Richmond, Victoria 3121, Australia
www.hardiegrantegmont.com.au

A CiP record for this title is available from the National Library of Australia

Sleepover Text copyright © 2005 Rowan McAuley
Birthday Girl Text copyright © 2006 Meredith Badger
Secret's Out Text copyright © 2008 Chrissie Perry
Music Mad Text copyright © 2007 Rowan McAuley
Flower Girl Text copyright © 2008 Chrissie Perry

Illustration and design copyright © 2013 Hardie Grant Egmont
The moral rights of the author have been asserted

Illustration by Aki Fukuoka
Design by Michelle Mackintosh
Text design and typesetting by Ektavo

Printed in Australia by Griffin Press, an Accredited ISO AS/NZS
14001:2004 Environmental Management System printer.

3 5 7 9 10 8 6 4 2

Contents

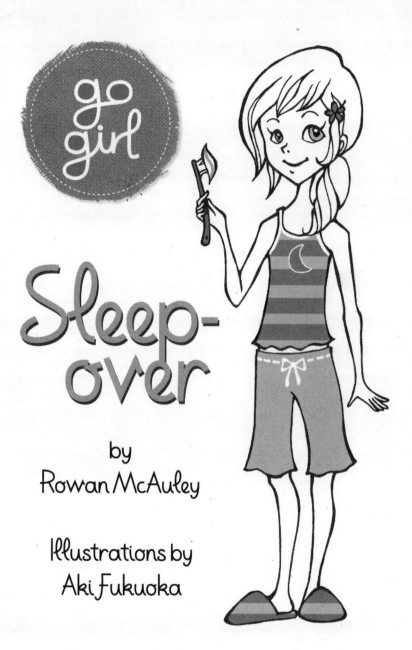

go girl

Sleep-over

by
Rowan McAuley

Illustrations by
Aki Fukuoka

Chapter One

It was six o'clock on Friday morning, the last day of school for the year. The alarm hadn't gone off yet, but Olivia was already awake and dressed and sitting at the kitchen table, eating her toast and waiting for her mum to get up.

She drank a glass of milk and ate an apple, but still her mum slept on. She brushed her teeth and made a sandwich for her lunch, but even then her mum did not stir.

Olivia checked the clock on the micro-wave. Six-thirty. Surely her mum should be awake by now? She tiptoed along the hallway and looked in. Her mum was fast asleep, snoring lightly. Olivia knocked gently on the open door. Her mum didn't move.

Olivia cleared her throat. 'Ahem!'

Her mum rolled over and snored more loudly. Olivia was getting desperate.

'Mum,' she whispered.

'Mum,' she said gently.

'Mum,' she said more firmly.

This was getting her nowhere.

'MUM!' she yelled suddenly, stamping her foot.

'Hmm?' said her mum, sitting up in bed, her hair all fluffy on one side. 'What's up, baby?'

'Mum,' said Olivia. 'You have to get up. I am sleeping over at Ching Ching's house tonight.'

'Are you?' said her mum. 'Are you sure? Did we talk about this?'

'Mum,' said Olivia sternly, because she had to be strict with her mum sometimes. 'You know we did. We talked about it on Monday, remember? You spoke with Mrs Adams on the phone.'

'I know, baby,' said her mum, yawning.

'I'm just teasing you.'

'Well,' said Olivia. 'Will you get up now?'

'Mm,' said her mum, still sounding tired. 'What time is it?'

'Six-thirty,' said Olivia. 'Or even later by now. We've been talking for at least five minutes.'

'Six-thirty?'

'Or six-thirty-five,' said Olivia.

'Is the sun even up yet?' asked her mum.

'Mum!'

'OK, OK,' said her mum. 'I'm getting up. Even though it's still the middle of the night,' she grumbled.

'Come on,' said Olivia. 'Here's your dressing gown.'

Hurry up, Mum, I'll be late!

While her mum had a shower, Olivia checked her bag. As well as her lunchbox, she had packed her pyjamas, her bathers, some clean clothes for tomorrow, her hairbrush, and a small box of chocolates for Ching Ching's mum, to say thank you. Was that everything?

It was almost seven o'clock and Olivia was dancing with impatience, waiting for her mum to finish blow-drying her hair. Finally she was ready.

'OK,' she said to Olivia. 'Now, are you sure you have packed everything you need?'

'Yes,' said Olivia.

'Pyjamas?'

'Yes,' said Olivia.

'Chocolates for Mrs Adams?'

'Yes,' said Olivia.

'Clean knickers for tomorrow?'

'Mum!'

'Well, have you?'

'YES!' said Olivia. 'Come on!'

'All right!' said her mum. 'Just checking.

I'll just get the house keys …'

But Olivia was already out the door and waiting at the front gate, her school bag on her back. Her mum locked the door and walked down the path (so slowly!) and together they walked to the bus stop.

'I'm going to miss you tonight,' said her mum.

'Yeah, yeah,' said Olivia, looking ahead for the bus.

'I will. I won't see you all day, I won't have anyone to eat dinner with, and you'll be at Ching Ching's until tomorrow …'

'I know,' said Olivia.

'What time am I picking you up?'

'Lunchtime,' said Olivia. 'Ching Ching

and I will have breakfast together, and play in the morning, and then you can pick me up at lunchtime.'

'Lunchtime it is,' said her mum, giving her a hug and a big smoochy kiss.

The bus was just arriving at the corner.

'Bye, Mum,' said Olivia, yelling back over her shoulder as she ran to catch it.

At last she was on her way.

Chapter Two

On the bus, Olivia tried to relax. She looked out the window and noticed how few cars there were on the road. She looked around the bus and saw all the empty seats. She wasn't going to be late at all. In fact, she was early.

It felt funny to sit on the same old bus, wearing her same old school uniform and carrying her same old school bag, knowing that inside the bag were her pink and green pyjamas. What if she got to school and Mrs Delano asked her to fetch something and she accidentally pulled out her new blue knickers instead?

She would die!

Or what if somebody found the box of chocolates for Ching Ching's mum and ate them, and she had nothing to give her? Or what if ...

Olivia was not very good at relaxing.

By the time the bus arrived outside school, she was exhausted. She had thought up a hundred different disasters and had worried about each and every one, and it wasn't even eight o'clock yet.

Olivia dragged her bag off the bus. She was starting to feel slightly sick.

Maybe it wasn't such a good idea to sleep over at Ching Ching's, even though they were best friends. What if she and Ching Ching had a fight and they weren't even friends by the time Ching Ching's mum came to pick them up from school? Maybe she should tell Ching Ching that she had changed her mind. She could just give the chocolates to Ching Ching, and then phone her mum and say she would come home for dinner after all.

Across the playground, she saw Ching Ching waving at her, a huge smile on her face. Ching Ching's mum was a teacher and her dad was a headmaster, so Ching Ching and her brothers were always at school early.

'Hi, Olivia!' said Ching Ching, running over. 'Isn't tonight going to be cool?'

'Yeah,' said Olivia, running to meet her halfway. 'It's going to be the best!'

She gave Ching Ching a hug, threw her

bag under a tree and they went to play with the other kids until the bell rang.

The last day of school always dragged on forever. Everyone was itching to get out and be on holidays, but first they had to empty their lockers, tidy up the class-room and collect all the art they had done that year.

Nobody could concentrate.

Dylan kept pestering Mrs Delano, asking, 'But why, Miss? It's the last day of school. Can't we just play?'

By lunchtime, Mrs Delano had given up.

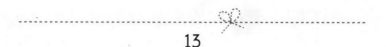

'OK,' she said. 'You win. We've done enough and it's too hot to work anyway.'

So they spent the rest of the day singing and talking about what everyone was doing for the holidays.

When home time came, everyone was lined up and ready to go. Bags on their shoulders, they crowded at the school gates, straining their ears for the bell.

Then the bell went and they were off, flying out to freedom. Some ran to buses, others went up the hill to the train station. Some walked home, and some, like Olivia and Ching Ching, waited to be picked up.

Ching Ching's parents both worked at the high school where Ching Ching's brothers went. Ching Ching was adopted and didn't look anything like her brothers. They were big, loud boys, all with the same short, spiky blond hair. Their names were Henry, Daniel and William.

Olivia had met them lots of times before, of course. The first time had been at Ching Ching's birthday party at the zoo. The boys were funny and rough, and had teased Ching Ching, picking her up and carrying her around the zoo, shouting to one another.

'Throw her to the seals!'

'No – too little! Not enough for a seal to eat. Here – catch!'

And Daniel had thrown – actually *thrown* – Ching Ching to Henry. Olivia had been astonished, watching her friend sail through the air like a doll. And Henry had caught her and called to William, 'Shall we chuck her to the monkeys?'

'Yeah!' said William. 'She looks like a monkey.'

'Smells like one, too,' said Daniel.

'Let's go!' said Henry, and all three boys

had carried Ching Ching away, hooting and chattering like monkeys as they went.

Olivia had been so upset, she was nearly in tears. How could they be so horrible to Ching Ching? And on her birthday!

But Ching Ching had come back giggling, sitting on William's shoulders and waving to everyone.

So they weren't bad boys, exactly. It's just that Olivia didn't have any brothers and wasn't quite sure what to make of them.

Chapter Three

'Hey!' said Ching Ching. 'There they are!'

She pointed to a car slowly driving by, looking for somewhere to park. Olivia could see that it was full of Ching Ching's brothers. Ching Ching's mum waved her hand out the driver's window.

'Come on,' said Ching Ching, and they ran to the car.

Mrs Adams parked the car a long, long

way up the street from the school. Ching Ching and Olivia were puffing by the time they got there.

It was a hot summer afternoon, and their school bags were heavy with all the things they had brought home from their desks and lockers. Olivia had her clothes for the sleep-over, too, so her bag was bulging at its zip.

Henry was sitting up the front next to Mrs Adams, and Daniel and William and their school bags were filling the back seat, so Ching Ching and Olivia decided to sit in the special backwards-facing seats in the car boot.

Olivia loved sitting back there, watching

the traffic come towards them, waving to the drivers in the cars behind as they waited at the lights. Mrs Adams opened the boot and helped them climb in.

'Hello, Olivia,' she said, after kissing Ching Ching.

'Hello, Mrs Adams,' said Olivia.

'Now,' said Mrs Adams. 'Did you remember everything?'

Standing behind her, Ching Ching rolled her eyes at Olivia. Olivia tried not to laugh.

'Yes, I think so,' said Olivia.

'Your pyjamas?' said Mrs Adams.

'Yes.'

'Your toothbrush?'

'Ye–,' Olivia began, but then stopped.

Her hand covered her mouth. Her eyes were as round as saucers. She felt herself blushing from her neck to her hair. She was horrified – she had forgotten her toothbrush.

'Oh no,' she said sadly.

'That's OK,' said Mrs Adams. 'I have to

stop at the shops on the way home anyway. We'll buy you a toothbrush there.'

'I'm so sorry,' said Olivia.

'It's no problem,' said Mrs Adams. 'You jump in with Ching Ching and we'll be off.'

Olivia was miserable. She had mucked up her sleep-over with Ching Ching even before they got to her house. How could she be so forgetful? How could she have left her toothbrush behind? She had been so careful with everything else. She felt like crying.

'Don't worry,' said Ching Ching. 'I always forget my toothbrush. That's why Mum asked.'

But it was too embarrassing and Olivia couldn't be cheered up. If only she knew that things were about to get worse!

Chapter Four

Mrs Adams pulled into the car park. All the kids streamed out. Mrs Adams sent Henry and William to the grocer's to buy some potatoes, green beans and broccoli. She sent Daniel to the supermarket to buy milk and rice, and she went with the girls to the chemist to pick up some tablets for Mr Adams and a toothbrush for Olivia. Ching Ching found a purple one with stars.

'You have to get this one, Mum,' she said. 'Please? I have a pink one and now Olivia and I can have the same.'

So Mrs Adams bought the toothbrush and they met the boys outside the butcher's. When the butcher saw them all standing there – Henry and William with the vegetables, Daniel with the milk and rice, and Mrs Adams with the girls – he looked amazed and said, 'What a lot of children!'

He leant over the counter and smiled at Olivia.

'And you're having a friend over to play! Aren't you lucky!' he said.

Oh, this was bad! Too, too terrible.

Olivia looked at Mrs Adams and her

long, blonde hair and light blue eyes. She looked at Henry, Daniel and William. They had blond hair and light blue eyes, too.

She looked at Ching Ching with her shiny black hair and dark brown eyes and realised that to strangers, Ching Ching did not look like she belonged. Instead, the butcher thought Olivia was Mrs Adams' daughter and Ching Ching was just a friend.

This was much, much worse than forgetting her toothbrush. Worse even than the thought of Henry, Daniel and William accidentally seeing her knickers.

She looked sideways at Ching Ching to see if she was angry, or if she was as upset and embarrassed as Olivia was, but Ching

Ching was looking at her mum with an odd smile on her face.

Mrs Adams looked at the butcher and said, 'What?!'

Mrs Adams hugged Ching Ching tightly to her.

'Only this one is mine,' she said loudly. 'I don't know where the rest of them came from.'

Ching Ching giggled in her mum's arms.

'Really?' said the butcher, looking surprised.

'Yes, it's true,' said Henry. 'We're all adopted, except for Ching Ching.'

'Oh,' said the butcher. 'Well. What can I get you?'

'Three kilos of sausages, please,' said Mrs Adams.

Back in the car, Olivia whispered to Ching Ching, 'That was awful.'

'Oh, we don't care,' laughed Ching Ching. 'It happens all the time. Mum made it into a game and now the boys compete to see who can say the silliest thing with a straight face. Henry always wins, of course.'

Chapter Five

Ching Ching's house was very different from Olivia's. At home, it was just Olivia and her mum. They lived in a small flat. They had one bedroom each, a sitting room where they ate their dinner off the coffee table in front of the TV, and a balcony where they hung their washing and grew herbs in pots. Everything was crowded but very neat.

Ching Ching's house was much bigger. There were four bedrooms. One for Mr and Mrs Adams, one for Henry, one that Daniel and William shared, and one for Ching Ching.

They had a huge kitchen and lounge room, and a big backyard with trees and a swimming pool.

There was lots of space, but everything was untidy and cluttered. There were books and papers on every surface, footballs and tennis balls and sports shoes all over the place, coffee mugs and pencil cases and calculators and toys and even bits of cold toast. It was a mess!

Olivia loved it. She was a quiet girl, but

secretly she loved all the noise and chaos of Ching Ching's house.

At her house, Olivia would have some fruit and yoghurt for afternoon tea, and then she would do her homework until her mum came home from work. Then they'd cook dinner together and watch TV.

At Ching Ching's house, Mrs Adams gave them biscuits and sponge cake for afternoon tea and sent them all outside. The boys played cricket and Olivia and Ching Ching swam in the pool until Mr Adams came home from being headmaster.

Then they all sat down to dinner at the dining table. At Olivia's house, her mum cooked spicy things like chilli beans and

curry, and they served up dinner straight from the pots on the stove. If Olivia wanted seconds she had to go back to the kitchen.

Mrs Adams cooked quite different food, in enormous pots. The food was laid out on the table in serving dishes and everyone helped themselves. That night they were having sausages, mashed potato, beans and broccoli.

The mashed potato was OK, and Olivia was used to beans and broccoli, but her mum never cooked sausages. Olivia really didn't like them, but Mrs Adams put three on her plate without asking, and now she had to eat them.

She looked around the table. Mr Adams and Henry were putting barbeque sauce on their sausages. Mrs Adams was sprinkling hers with salt and pepper. Ching Ching was having tomato sauce.

'Do you want some?' she asked Olivia.

'Yes, please,' said Olivia.

She liked tomato sauce, and maybe if she had enough of it she could get through the sausages. She took the bottle from

Ching Ching. It was a big bottle, but it was nearly empty and the sauce was taking forever to trickle out. Olivia shook it gently over her plate.

Nothing.

She shook it again.

'Where's the tomato sauce?' said Daniel.

'Olivia's using it,' said Ching Ching.

'Hurry up,' said Daniel, rolling his eyes.

Olivia blushed. She could feel everyone looking at her and the stupid bottle of sauce. The sauce still hadn't come out.

'Daniel,' said Mr Adams. 'Don't be so rude. Take your time, Olivia. Daniel's in no hurry.'

'Yes, I am,' said Daniel. 'I'm starving.

Look, just give the bottle a good thump,'
he said to Olivia.

Olivia wished she'd never come. Or
that Daniel would shut up. Or at the very
least, that the sauce would come out!

She hit the bottle hard, and then –
SPLAT!

A huge dollop of sauce spurted out
of the bottle all over her plate, making
a disgusting sound. It covered all three
sausages, all the beans, and most of the
mashed potato.

'Oh, come on!' said Daniel. 'Have you
left any for us?'

'Daniel!' said Mr Adams. 'Enough!'

Ching Ching poked her tongue out at

her brother. Olivia passed him the sauce, not even looking at him.

'But, Dad,' said Daniel. 'You never let us have that much sauce. You always say we can only have a dab.'

Olivia just wanted to disappear.

Dinner was a disaster.

She tried to pretend that she liked having great pools of sauce all over her food. She cut up the first sausage and ate a piece. It was dripping with sauce. *It's not too bad*, she told herself.

The boys were talking to their dad, and Ching Ching was telling her mum about school, so no-one was left to talk to Olivia. Good. She kept her head down and worked through the sausages, covering each bite in sauce.

By the time she finished her dinner, she felt ill. She never wanted to taste tomato sauce again. Her throat was burning with it. More than anything in the world, Olivia wanted her mum to phone up and say she needed Olivia back home right away.

'Has everyone had enough to eat?' said Mrs Adams.

'That was great,' said Mr Adams.

William groaned and patted his belly. Henry burped.

'Henry!' said Mrs Adams. 'Olivia, dear, would you like some more?'

Olivia shook her head firmly. *No way*, she thought.

'I mean, no thanks,' she said, trying to sound polite.

'Right, then,' said Mrs Adams. 'Clear the table.'

The Adams had no television, but they did have a dishwasher. After dinner, each person rinsed their own plate and stacked it in the dishwasher.

When the table was cleared, Mrs Adams brought a tub of ice-cream and a packet of waffle cones to the table.

'One ice-cream cone each,' she said. 'And you can eat them outside.'

She made up the cones and passed them one by one along the table.

'Now, shoo!' she said. 'I need some peace and quiet.'

Chapter Six

Outside it was still light. The sun was setting, though, and the sky was pink and orange over the trees.

Henry, Daniel and William ate their ice-creams as fast as they could and went back to playing cricket. Ching Ching and Olivia made their ice-creams last as long as possible and then decided to go for another swim.

'It's so nice to swim as it gets dark,' said Ching Ching. 'The water's so warm, and you can just lie on your back and watch the bats go by and the stars come out.'

Olivia agreed. They paddled and talked and looked at the sky and, except for the boys shouting as they played cricket, it was very peaceful.

After a while, it was too dark for the boys to see the ball and they packed up and went back inside. It was really quiet by the pool now, and a tiny bit spooky.

'Do you ever think,' said Olivia, 'you could just sink under the water and never come up?'

'Yeah,' said Ching Ching. 'You could

swim so deep you got sucked down that
big plug hole.'

They shuddered happily at the thought.
They did this sometimes – talked about
scary things to see how badly they could
frighten themselves.

'And the next day, there'd be nothing

but your pigtail stuck in the pool filter,' said Olivia.

'And then one foot would be washed up on a beach, miles and miles away,' said Ching Ching.

'Eew!' they said together, laughing, but holding tight onto the edge of the pool, just in case.

'We should sleep out here tonight,' said Ching Ching.

'Yeah?' said Olivia. 'What about the mosquitoes?'

'We would be OK under the sheets,' said Ching Ching. 'Maybe we could burn one of those smelly candles, too.'

'And we could stay up all night and

watch the sunrise,' said Olivia.

'Ching Ching!'

It was Mrs Adams calling from the back door.

'Time for bed. You and Olivia, out of the pool, now!'

'You can *so* tell your mum is a school teacher,' said Olivia.

They got out of the pool and found that their fingers and toes had gone wrinkly. The air was cool on their wet skin and by the time they got inside they were shivering.

They stood together in front of the bathroom mirror with their matching toothbrushes, giggling and trying to brush their chattering teeth. They brushed their hair and Ching Ching tied hers back in long, low plaits for bed. They changed into their pyjamas and decided it was too much effort to sleep outside that night.

Ching Ching had bunk beds, and because it was the first time Olivia had slept over, she got to sleep on the top.

'I always read for a bit before I go to sleep,' said Ching Ching. 'Would you like to borrow a book, or do you have one?'

'Borrow one, please,' said Olivia, because Ching Ching always had heaps of books. Olivia supposed it was because both her parents were teachers.

Olivia found one about a girl who ran

away to sea on a pirate ship. It looked very interesting, but when she climbed up the ladder to her bed and got in under the covers, she didn't feel like reading.

At home, in her own bed, her mum usually came in and kissed her goodnight. Sometimes they talked about their day, sometimes Olivia read out loud from a book, and sometimes her mum told her a story instead. She remembered how her mum had said that morning that she would miss Olivia.

Olivia realised this was the first time she had ever gone to bed without even a hug from her mum. She felt a bit sad and lonely.

Outside in the pool, talking with Ching Ching, Olivia had forgotten all about the embarrassment of dinner. Now, lying in bed, she started thinking about it all over again. She felt her stomach shrink into a cold, hard ball.

It was too late to call her mum and ask to go home. She was stuck here. Daniel was

horrible, Mrs Adams probably thought she was stupid for forgetting her toothbrush, and everyone thought she was greedy for eating all that tomato sauce.

How could she sleep with all these thoughts in her head? She wanted to cry but she didn't want Ching Ching to hear her. In the bunk below, Ching Ching switched off her lamp.

'Goodnight, Olivia,' she said.

'Goodnight,' said Olivia, hoping her voice sounded normal.

Olivia turned off her lamp, too. The room was very dark now. How long until morning? Olivia rolled onto her side and pretended she was in her own bed. She imagined her own room, her own toys, her own blankets over her. She imagined her mum in the room next door, and it must have worked because very soon she was fast asleep.

Chapter Seven

Olivia had strange dreams. She woke up suddenly, and for a moment she couldn't work out where she was. The bed was on the wrong side of the window, and up too high, and her pillow smelt funny. It was still dark. She could hear a clock ticking and someone below her breathing.

Oh yes – she was at Ching Ching's house. She couldn't remember her dream but she

felt wide awake. What time was it? It was definitely too early to get up.

At home she would have gone to the toilet and then maybe crept into her mum's bed for a cuddle until morning.

That wasn't a good thing to think about right now. It just made her feel sorry for herself. Instead, she would think of warm, sleepy things. Hot chocolate before bedtime, sheepskin slippers, the sound of heavy rain on the roof …

When Olivia opened her eyes again, it was properly Saturday morning. The sunlight was bright through Ching Ching's curtains and the bedcovers felt too warm now.

Olivia listened. The house was still very quiet. Not sleeping quiet, but empty quiet.

She peered over the edge of her bunk bed and looked for Ching Ching. Her bed was a tumble of blankets and sheets, but there was no Ching Ching in it.

Olivia couldn't decide whether to get

up or stay where she was and wait for Ching Ching to come back. Would it be worse to lie in bed for ages and have Ching Ching waiting for her, or worse to go down the hallway and bump into Henry or Daniel or William while she was wearing her pink and green pyjamas?

She was sitting up in bed, the top of her head almost brushing the ceiling, when Ching Ching appeared at the doorway.

'Oh, you're up,' she said. 'Good. We have the house to ourselves.'

'Where's everyone gone?' asked Olivia.

'The boys play sport on Saturday, so Dad's taken Henry to one field, and Mum has taken Daniel and William to another.

They'll be back for lunch, though.'

Phew! Olivia could avoid horrible Daniel at least until lunchtime. She climbed down from the bed.

'The boys have eaten all the good cereal,' said Ching Ching. 'There's only bread left for us.'

'Are you allowed to use the stove?' asked Olivia.

'Probably,' said Ching Ching. 'Why?'

'I could make us French toast. Mum and I make it all the time.'

'Cool,' said Ching Ching. 'That's way better than cereal. What do you need?'

'Eggs, milk and butter,' said Olivia. 'And a frypan. And bread, of course.'

Olivia set about mixing the eggs and milk and soaking the bread.

'While I'm making this,' she said, 'you should find some cinnamon sugar to go with it.'

Ching Ching looked.

'We don't have any,' she said.

'Maple syrup?'

'Nope,' said Ching Ching. 'What about honey?'

'That will work,' said Olivia, dropping the first slice of bread into the frypan. It sizzled nicely.

'We've got bananas and strawberries, too,' said Ching Ching.

'Perfect,' said Olivia, turning the toast.

In the end, it was a beautiful breakfast. Olivia cooked them two slices of French toast each, and Ching Ching decorated the toast with honey and fruit.

'Wait,' said Ching Ching. 'One more thing.'

She pulled a can of whipped cream out

of the fridge and squirted a long squiggle onto each plate.

'That,' said Olivia, 'is so fancy.'

'Yeah,' said Ching Ching.

'Almost too fancy to eat.'

'Yeah,' said Ching Ching.

They were quiet for a second, admiring their work. Then Ching Ching caught Olivia's eye and smiled.

'No,' she said. 'I can eat it.'

'Me too,' said Olivia.

They sat by the pool, dangling their legs in the water and eating the toast off plates balanced on their laps.

'This is so nice,' said Olivia.

'Yeah,' said Ching Ching. 'I wish we could do this every Saturday. No boys yelling, no parents nagging.'

'Is it nice having a big family?' asked Olivia.

'Mostly. I get tired of being the smallest sometimes, though.'

Olivia was the biggest and the smallest rolled into one in her family, but she understood what Ching Ching meant.

'Still,' she said. 'I bet you don't get bored.'

'No,' said Ching Ching, eating the last strawberry on her plate.

There was a loud bang from the house as the front door slammed shut. Then Mrs Adams called out from the back door, 'Ching Ching!'

'Oh, no,' said Ching Ching. 'They're back already and we haven't even had our Saturday morning skinny dip yet.'

Chapter Eight

'Ching Ching,' said Mrs Adams, when they were back inside the house. 'Have you been using the stove?'

Olivia froze.

In her hands were the dirty plates from breakfast, and in the kitchen, sitting in the sink, was the dirty frypan she had used to cook the French toast.

'No,' said Ching Ching.

Olivia couldn't believe her ears. Mrs Adams looked angry. No, more than angry. She looked wild and fierce.

'Ching Ching,' said Mrs Adams. 'Don't lie to me. Have you been using the stove?'

'I promise,' said Ching Ching. 'I never touched the stove. Did I, Olivia?'

Mrs Adams turned to Olivia, and Olivia was so frightened she could hardly breathe.

'Is Ching Ching telling the truth?' asked Mrs Adams.

'Yes,' said Olivia in a shaky voice.

'See?' said Ching Ching to her mum.

'Well, then,' said Mrs Adams. 'Who made all this mess?'

'I don't know,' said Ching Ching.

She was about to say more, but Olivia spoke up.

'*I* did,' Olivia said.

She didn't know what would happen to her now, but she couldn't keep quiet. She would rather die than have Mrs Adams angry with her, but she never lied to her mum and didn't know how *not* to tell the truth.

'I used the stove,' she said quietly.

Mrs Adams looked at her. Ching Ching stared at her.

'*You*, Olivia?' said Mrs Adams.

'I cooked French toast,' said Olivia.

She looked at Ching Ching, but her friend's face was a careful blank.

'I see,' said Mrs Adams. 'Didn't Ching

Ching tell you she isn't allowed to use the stove without a grown-up in the house?'

Olivia shook her head.

'I mean,' she said quickly, not wanting to get Ching Ching in trouble, 'she thought perhaps it might be all right.'

Mrs Adams sighed and looked at the two of them.

'I'm sorry to say this, Olivia,' she said. 'But Ching Ching did not tell you the truth. In this house, children are not allowed to cook on their own.'

'I'm sorry,' said Olivia, almost in a whisper.

'Ching Ching,' said Mrs Adams. 'I'm so angry with you right now. Did you know the stove was left on? When I came in, the hot plate was glowing red. That's how fires start, and houses burn down, and people get very badly hurt.'

Ching Ching said nothing.

'Well, what do you have to say for yourself?' asked Mrs Adams.

'The boys ate all the good cereal,' said Ching Ching. 'There was nothing else for us to eat.'

'That's not quite true, is it?' said Mrs Adams. 'You could have used the toaster. Or the microwave. You could have had banana sandwiches, or made milkshakes. You weren't going to starve.'

Mrs Adams opened the fridge to show Ching Ching all the things she could have had for breakfast.

'Look,' she said. 'Orange juice, water-melon, cheese, tomatoes. You could have had – hey! Did you eat all the strawberries?'

Oh no, thought Olivia.

'Right,' said Mrs Adams, slamming the

fridge. 'Go to your room now, Ching Ching!
I'm just furious.'

The two girls fled.

Chapter Nine

In Ching Ching's room, Olivia finally started to breathe again.

'I thought your mum was going to kill us,' she said.

'She would have if you'd kept talking,' said Ching Ching.

'Me?' said Olivia. 'What did I do?'

'Only told her everything,' said Ching Ching. 'If you'd kept quiet we'd be outside right now, having a swim.'

Olivia was shocked.

'What are you talking about?' she said.
'I left the stove on and we weren't even
meant to touch it!'

'So?' said Ching Ching.

'And you lied to your mum!'

'Sort of,' said Ching Ching. 'But it wasn't
a big lie.'

Olivia stared at her friend. She thought
Ching Ching was crazy to lie to Mrs Adams.

Ching Ching sighed.

'Look,' she said. 'You don't have any
brothers or sisters, so you probably don't
understand. When you have a big family,
you don't need to get into trouble. Mum

and Dad are so busy, and there are so many of us, you can just do what you like. As long as everyone keeps quiet, Mum and Dad can never work out who did what and so no-one gets the blame.'

'That's terrible,' said Olivia, but she could see that it was a bit exciting too.

'But you dobbed us in, so now we have to sit here,' said Ching Ching.

'Your mum would have known it was us, though,' said Olivia. 'We were the only ones home.'

'Probably,' said Ching Ching. 'But then maybe she left with Daniel and William before Dad and Henry left, so maybe it wasn't us after all.'

Olivia thought about her place, with just her and her mum. Her mum could tell exactly what Olivia did – every dropped sock, every wet towel, every crumb on the coffee table. Who else could it be?

It was hard to imagine what it would be like to live in Ching Ching's house. You could get away with so many things!

On the other hand, maybe that made it lonely sometimes. Olivia liked the idea that her mum knew everything about her.

'Anyway,' said Ching Ching. 'It was worth it. That was the best breakfast I've ever had.'

'You're a shocker,' said Olivia.

'I know,' said Ching Ching. 'I'm really, really naughty. But guess what? I'm also full of French toast and strawberries, and I don't care.'

Olivia laughed. She couldn't help it. Ching Ching really was terrible, but she was so funny too. Olivia knew they were stuck in Ching Ching's room because they

were in disgrace, but right now, giggling
with her best friend, even that seemed
kind of fun.

Chapter Ten

They stayed in Ching Ching's room for ages, reading books and playing with Ching Ching's toys. They heard Mr Adams come home with Henry, and then all three brothers and Mr Adams went outside for a swim. Ching Ching and Olivia watched them from the bedroom window.

The boys were diving and bombing into the pool and water was splashing up in waves all over the sides. Mr Adams was sitting on the steps in the shallow end, the water up to his chest, cheering the boys on.

'Well done, William!' he called. 'That was the biggest bomb yet. Watch out, Henry! Daniel's in your way.'

'I'm bored now,' said Ching Ching. 'Don't you think we've been stuck in here long enough?'

'Maybe,' said Olivia doubtfully.

In fact, she felt safe in Ching Ching's room. Outside, Mrs Adams was cross with them, and Daniel might embarrass her again. Who knew what other trouble was waiting?

In here she had Ching Ching all to

herself, and they could play until her mum came to take her home.

'We could do another magazine quiz,' she said, but Ching Ching was already opening the bedroom door.

The smell of frying onions drifted in and Ching Ching stood with her head in the hallway, sniffing deeply.

'Oh,' she said with longing. 'Hamburgers. My favourite.'

It seemed like a long time since breakfast and Olivia's stomach growled.

'I'd love a hamburger,' she said. 'But my mum's coming to pick me up soon.'

'Before lunch or after?' asked Ching Ching.

'I'm not sure.'

'But you will stay for hamburgers, won't you?'

'I hope so,' said Olivia, because the smell was getting stronger and more delicious every minute.

'Oops,' said Ching Ching, jumping back inside the room and shutting the door. 'Mum's coming.'

They scurried onto Ching Ching's bed and pretended to be reading books just as Mrs Adams opened the door.

'OK, you two,' she said. 'Lunchtime. Olivia, do you know what time your mum is coming to pick you up?'

'No,' said Olivia.

'Well, you've got time for a burger, anyway. Your mum can join us if she gets here early. And then,' she said more sternly, looking at Ching Ching and the mess in her bedroom, 'you can come back here and tidy up a bit.'

Lunch was actually quite fun. They put their hamburgers together on the dining table. Olivia tried to make sure Daniel was nowhere near when she got her burger, and she avoided the tomato sauce too!

She was just putting some lettuce on her bun and trying to decide whether to have beetroot and cheese when someone beside her said, 'Do you want some lemonade?'

Olivia looked up and froze. It was Daniel, pouring lemonade into plastic cups. Was he teasing her? Was he being rude somehow? What should she say? Daniel just smiled and passed her a cup.

'Thanks,' said Olivia. She didn't know what else to say.

Thanks!

She suddenly thought that maybe it didn't really matter about the tomato sauce after all.

She went out with her burger and found Ching Ching sitting under a tree, already eating.

Olivia realised her sleep-over was almost over. Part of her felt glad. It would be nice to be back home where she knew all the rules and liked all the food.

Another part of her, though, felt sad because she would miss Ching Ching. She would even miss the things that frightened her – Mrs Adams when she was angry, Daniel, and the brave and lonely feeling she had sleeping on the top bunk.

Mr Adams called down from the back door. 'Olivia! Look who's here!'

Olivia looked up, and there was her mum. She looked very short next to Mr Adams, and Olivia had forgotten how pretty she was.

'Oh, bum,' said Ching Ching. 'Now you'll have to go home, I suppose.'

'Yeah,' said Olivia, and she couldn't tell if she was happy or sad.

They wandered back towards the house.

'Hi, Mum,' said Olivia.

'Hi, baby,' said her mum.

Olivia didn't want to hug her in front of everybody. Luckily her mum seemed to know this.

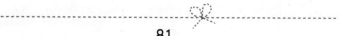

'Have you had a good time?' asked her mum.

'Yeah,' said Olivia.

'Have you behaved yourself?'

'Um, yeah,' said Olivia, looking sideways at Mrs Adams.

Mrs Adams laughed.

'She's been a peach,' she said. 'They've been up to a few tricks, but nothing too terrible.'

Olivia smiled with relief.

'Have you packed?' said her mum.

'Not yet.'

'Go on, then. I'll stay and chat with Mrs Adams while you do.'

In Ching Ching's room, Olivia found

Thanks for having me.

the box of chocolates as she packed her pyjamas.

'Oh, I forgot to give these to your mum,' she said.

'Let's keep them,' said Ching Ching. 'Or we could tell Mum she can only have them if she promises you can sleep over next weekend.'

'Or you could sleep over at my house,' said Olivia. 'I could make French toast again for breakfast.'

Ching Ching dragged Olivia's bag to the front door. For some reason it didn't seem to zip up as well as it had the day before. Olivia's pink and green pyjamas stuck out the top, but now she didn't care who saw them.

'Thank you for having me,' she said to Mrs Adams, giving her the chocolates.

'Oh, lovely,' said Mrs Adams. 'These will be even better than strawberries after dinner tonight.'

Olivia blushed. She took her bag from Ching Ching and followed her mum out the front door.

'Bye,' she said, waving.

She felt happy and brave and somehow more grown up than yesterday.

'I'm glad you had fun,' said her mum as they got into the car.

'Yes,' said Olivia. 'I really did.'

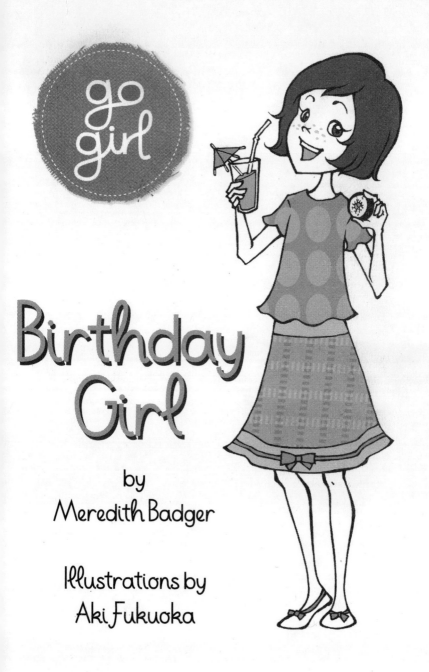

go girl

Birthday Girl

by
Meredith Badger

Illustrations by
Aki Fukuoka

Chapter One

Annabelle was lying on her bed, feeling terrible. She felt terrible even though it was the weekend. She felt terrible even though it was a beautiful, sunny day. And she felt terrible even though it was her birthday party.

In fact, her birthday party was the main reason she felt so bad.

I'm staying in here until it's all over and

everyone's gone home, thought Annabelle. *And I'm never*, ever *having a party again.*

Usually Annabelle loved having parties. Her birthday was in summer and she always had a party in her backyard. Each year there was a different theme.

One year it was 'Hawaiian'. Everyone wore grass skirts and long necklaces made of flowers, and they drank tropical juice out of coconut shells.

Another year the theme was 'winter' and they pretended it was really cold instead of really hot. There were huge fake icebergs on the lawn and Annabelle's Uncle Bob had made an excellent life-size snowman out of foam.

Then last year she had a 'school pool' party. Her friends all wore their school uniforms and brought their school bags. There had even been lessons … but fun ones! In one class they made pizzas. And in another class they decorated T-shirts with glitter paint. Then they all jumped into Annabelle's pool.

So Annabelle had always been pretty sure she knew what made a good party. But that all changed the day she went to her best friend Nicole's party.

Usually Nicole had an at-home party, too. But this time she'd had it at a rock-climbing centre.

Nicole had invited the school gang – Dani, Chloe, Sarah, Lola and Annabelle. But she'd invited lots of other people, too. Most of their class went, even the boys. Some of Nicole's new basketball friends were also there.

For lunch they'd had wedges and nachos at the centre's cafe. Then Nicole's mum pulled out a big pink and gold box. Inside was a huge cake from the bakery, decorated with chocolate curls. Written on the top in pink icing was, 'Happy Birthday Nicole'. It was the most beautiful cake Annabelle had ever seen.

'This cake is awesome,' said Dani, as they each munched on a slice. 'In fact, this is one of the best parties I've ever been to. Rock-climbing is cool fun.'

'Yeah,' agreed Chloe. 'I wish we could come here for every party!'

'Was it a good party, Belly?' asked her mum when she picked her up afterwards.

'It was soooo much fun!' said Annabelle, grinning.

Then she looked at her mum. She had something to ask. It was *her* birthday soon. And she wanted her party to be just as good as Nicole's had been.

'Mum,' Annabelle said nervously, 'could I have a rock-climbing party, too?'

'I thought you liked having parties at home,' said her mum, surprised.

Annabelle felt a bit bad. She knew her mum and Uncle Bob always put a lot of

effort into her parties. And until now she'd thought her parties were great. But she couldn't help feeling that Nicole's party had been heaps better. A normal backyard party suddenly seemed like something for little kids. But there was no way Annabelle could say that to her mum.

'Home parties are great, Mum,' said Annabelle, in the end. 'I just feel like doing something different this year.'

Annabelle's mum frowned. This meant she was thinking.

'OK,' she said, after a minute. 'You can have a rock-climbing party.'

'Yay!' said Annabelle, bouncing on her seat with excitement.

'Hang on,' said her mum. 'There's a *but*.'

Annabelle groaned.

Buts were never good.

'If you have a party at home you can invite whoever you want. But if you have a rock-climbing party you can only invite three people.'

'Only *three*?' said Annabelle.

That was a big *but*.

One of the reasons Nicole's party had

been so good was because there were heaps of kids there. It wouldn't be the same with just three.

But Annabelle's mum was firm.

'That's the deal,' she said. 'Now it's up to you to decide.'

Chapter Two

By Sunday, Annabelle still hadn't decided what to do. It would be so awesome to have a rock-climbing party. But how would she choose who to take? There was her bestie Nicole, for a start. Plus she had her second besties – Sarah, Dani, Chloe and Lola.

Then there were her orchestra friends. Annabelle had been playing in the orchestra for a while now and she really liked Siri and Freya. And what about the kids who lived nearby? She always invited Michiko from next door and Shae who lived down the road. Plus there was no way she could leave out Sophie, who was her friend as well as her cousin.

It was just way too hard to pick only three friends.

As Annabelle lay on her bed thinking, her mum stuck her head around the door.

'Come on, Belly. It's time for lunch at Uncle Bob's,' she said.

Annabelle and her mum had lunch at Uncle Bob's place every Sunday. Sometimes Sophie was there, too. But some Sundays she was at her mum's place.

'Cool,' said Annabelle, getting up.

She liked going to Uncle Bob's. He was an illustrator and had lots of funny drawings stuck up around the house. And this week Sophie would be there.

I can ask her what she'd do about this whole party thing, thought Annabelle. Her cousin was good at solving problems.

Sophie was using the computer when they arrived. She listened as Annabelle explained her problem.

'I think your parties are cool the way they are,' said Sophie. 'But it's up to you, I guess.' Then she typed something into the computer. 'Let's visit the Party Princess website. She might be able to help.'

Seconds later a girl appeared on the screen wearing a tiara and holding a present.

'That's the Party Princess,' explained Sophie. 'She knows everything there is to know about parties.'

Sophie clicked on the WHAT'S HOT section.

Party Princess

★WHAT'S HOT RIGHT NOW? MOCKTAIL PARTIES!

- *Wear your best clothes*
- *Serve brightly coloured soft drinks and juices in tall glasses*
- *Offer unusual snacks on silver trays*
- *Play croquet*

Annabelle grinned.

'That's it!' she said. 'I'll have a mocktail party! Then I can invite whoever I like. And it'll also be totally different to the sort of parties I usually have.'

Sophie nodded.

'Cool idea, Bell,' she said.

Over lunch, Annabelle explained her idea to her mum and Uncle Bob.

'Everyone can dress up. We can have fancy drinks in tall glasses and food on silver trays,' she said excitedly. 'Then we can all play *crock-kwit*.'

Her mum frowned for a moment. Then she laughed.

'You mean *croquet*,' she said, saying it

'croak-ay'. 'I wonder how you play it?'

Annabelle's face fell. She had hoped her mum would know.

'You're all forgetting the most important question!' said Uncle Bob suddenly. 'What sort of invitations should we make?'

Annabelle bit her lip.

Uncle Bob made Annabelle's party invitations every year. For the Hawaiian party he made girls who wiggled their hips when you pulled a tab. For the winter party he'd drawn penguins wearing sparkly hats. And for the school party he'd made invitations that looked like report cards.

But Nicole's birthday invitations had come from a proper party shop. They had gold edges and smelt like watermelon. Annabelle really wanted invitations like that this year. But before she could say anything Uncle Bob slapped the table.

'I know!' he said. 'We can make them look like cocktail glasses! And as you pull the straw the drink will disappear.'

Annabelle sighed, but very quietly. There was no way she could say anything now. Uncle Bob was way too excited.

After lunch they all set to work on the invitations. Uncle Bob designed them on the computer. Then Sophie, who was almost as good as Uncle Bob on the computer, coloured them in. Then they printed them out and everyone helped put them together. As a final touch Annabelle added red and gold glitter to the straws.

It took all afternoon but the time passed quickly. Uncle Bob kept drawing funny things in the glasses. In one he drew a dolphin wearing goggles. And in another he added a duck doing backstroke.

When the invitations were finished Sophie spread them out over the table.

'They look so cool!' she said.

Annabelle nodded.

They *did* look good. And seeing them there made her realise that her birthday was very soon! Annabelle felt all quivery just thinking about it.

This is going to be the coolest party I've ever had, she thought.

Chapter Three

'Excellent invitation, Bell!' said Sarah, a few days later. 'But how come you're not having a pool party? Your school pool party was the best.'

'I just wanted to do something different this year,' explained Annabelle. 'Pool parties are boring.'

'I don't think they're boring,' said Dani. 'Yours was awesome.'

Annabelle smiled. She thought Dani was probably just saying that to be nice.

'What should we wear?' asked Dani.

Annabelle thought for a moment.

'Something really dressy,' she replied.

'I'll borrow some clothes from my sister,' said Dani excitedly. 'She'll have something for sure.'

'Good idea,' nodded Chloe. 'What will you wear, Bell?'

Usually Annabelle wore a good top with her favourite jeans or a skirt to parties. For her school pool party she had worn her school uniform over the top of her bathers. For Nicole's rock-climbing party she'd worn leggings and a T-shirt.

But none of these things would be right for a mocktail party. She needed something really special.

'I still haven't decided yet,' Annabelle shrugged. 'But it'll be cool.'

Then she turned to Nicole.

'What about you, Nic?' she said.

But Nicole was looking at the invitation with a big frown on her face.

It's like she's not one bit excited, thought Annabelle, feeling hurt.

'The party is on the 12th?' asked Nicole, looking worried.

'Yep,' replied Annabelle. 'It starts at two o'clock. Why?'

Nicole twiddled with her ponytail. She

always did that when something was bothering her.

'Well, the Cockatoos won the semi-final,' she explained. 'So now we're in the grand final.'

Nicole had recently started playing basketball.

Annabelle gave her friend a hug.

'That's so great! But how come you look like you've just been given detention?'

Nicole sighed.

'The grand final is on the 12th.'

Annabelle stared at Nicole.

'You mean, you're not coming to my party?' she asked, her jaw dropping.

'Of *course* I'm coming,' said Nicole

quickly. 'I'll just be a bit late, that's all.'

Annabelle's heart sank.

She didn't know what to say. Nicole had been to every one of her parties since they were three. She was usually the first to arrive and the last to leave. She had always been in charge of choosing the music. And somehow she always managed to pick songs that everyone liked.

Who would do the music until she arrived?

Then there was the Happy Birthday song. Nicole always sang it the loudest. And she was the one who said, 'Hip hip!' so that everyone else could say, 'Hooray!'

If she wasn't there, would someone else remember to do it?

Just then the recess bell rang and the gang headed back to class.

Annabelle and Nicole walked side by side, but without talking. Annabelle's mind was whirling around.

Maybe I could change the party to a different day, she thought. But it was too late to do that. Most of the invitations had been sent out already.

Then Annabelle had a really horrible thought. It was so horrible that she screwed up her face and tried to shake it out of her head. But when she stopped shaking the thought was still there.

Maybe Nic doesn't want to come to my party. I bet if I was having a rock-climbing party she would miss her basketball game.

Annabelle and Nicole arrived at their classroom. Annabelle sat down, feeling terrible. Out of the corner of her eye she could see Nicole watching her. Nicole looked like she wanted to say something, but just then their teacher walked in.

'Quiet, everyone,' Mr Clarke said. 'No talking please!'

But the moment he turned around, Nicole grabbed Annabelle's hand under the desk and squeezed it tightly.

'Don't worry, Bell,' she whispered. 'After the game I'm going to change into my fastest running shoes and run the whole way to your place.'

Annabelle couldn't help smiling.

'The basketball court is about twenty blocks away from my place,' she whispered back. 'You can't run all that way!'

'Well, my dad will probably give me a lift,' admitted Nicole. 'But if we get stuck in a traffic jam I'm going to jump out and run the rest of the way. I don't want to miss any more of your party than I have to!'

'Nicole!' said Mr Clarke, turning around. 'What did I say about talking?'

'Sorry, Mr Clarke,' said Nicole.

But when he turned back she grinned at Annabelle.

'I'll be there in time for the cake,' she promised.

Annabelle grinned back. She felt much better. Of course Nicole wanted to come to her party! It was just really bad luck that the grand final was on the same day.

But at least now Annabelle was sure that her friend would get there as soon as she possibly could.

Chapter Four

After school, Annabelle had orchestra practice. Her friends Siri and Freya were already there when she arrived. Siri played the viola and Freya played cello. Annabelle played violin. She'd been learning for over a year now.

Playing in the orchestra was good fun. At the moment everyone was practising really hard because they had a concert coming up. It was at the town hall and everyone had to wear their best clothes to perform.

Annabelle had gone shopping with her mum to buy a special outfit. They bought a purple skirt with a pink ribbon around the bottom and a silky pink shirt to match. They also bought some cute shoes with bows.

Annabelle always concentrated really hard when she was playing in the orchestra. She knew all the violin parts really well because she practised them at home. But there were more things to think about when she played with everyone else. She had to follow the music on the page and

make sure she knew which bit they were up to, even when she wasn't playing. Otherwise she might miss her cue to start.

After they had played through all the pieces, Mrs Bailey clapped.

'Good work, everyone,' she said. 'The strings section sounded particularly good.'

Siri, Freya and Annabelle all grinned proudly at each other.

They were in the strings section!

During the break, Annabelle pulled out the last two party invitations.

'These are for you,' she said.

'Cool!' said Freya, looking at hers. 'I've never been to a mocktail party before. Do you still play games and stuff?'

'Um ...' said Annabelle.

She hadn't really thought about the games yet. At all her other parties they had played things like musical chairs and the chocolate game.

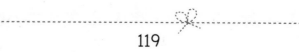

At her school pool party they had played party games in the pool. Even pass the parcel! Annabelle's mum had wrapped each layer of the parcel in a plastic bag so it didn't get soggy. Everyone agreed afterwards that playing it in the pool was even more fun.

But Siri and Freya were a little bit older than her other friends. They might think that those games were for little kids.

Then Annabelle remembered what the Party Princess had said.

'We're going to play croquet!' she said.

Annabelle still wasn't really sure what croquet was. But it sounded like a grown-up type of game.

'Oh, and guess what?' Annabelle added. 'All the food is going to be served on silver platters!'

'How excellent!' said Siri. 'What kind of food?'

'I'm not sure yet,' admitted Annabelle. 'But it won't be anything baby-ish.'

'I can't wait!' smiled Freya. 'It sounds totally cool!'

Annabelle nodded.

'Yep, it will be,' she said.

At least, I hope it will be, she thought.

During the second part of orchestra practice, Annabelle didn't play nearly so well. She missed her cues. And she played some wrong notes, too. The problem was that her head was full of party thoughts now. Like, how was she going to find out about croquet? And what kind of food should she serve?

Then, during the final piece, Annabelle thought of something else.

What if my friends don't get along?

The same people had been coming to her parties for years. They all knew each other. But Freya and Siri had never met them before.

What if Freya and Siri don't get along with my other friends? worried Annabelle. *They are older than everyone else. And they probably like totally different music, too.*

But it was too late to change anything now. All Annabelle could do was cross her fingers and hope that everyone got along.

Chapter Five

'This afternoon I'll take you shopping for party food,' said Annabelle's mum when she dropped her off at school the next day. 'Make a list of what we'll need.'

Usually buying the party food was simple. They bought party pies, sausage rolls, cocktail frankfurts, chips and lollies. Her mum made mini-pizzas and Annabelle helped make chocolate crackles.

Sometimes they had extra things, depending on the party's theme. For the Hawaiian party there were pineapple and marshmallow skewers. For her winter party there were snowballs and rainbow icy poles. And for the school party her mum had made everyone a lunchbag with fairy bread sandwiches in them.

Then they had cake.

Annabelle's mum had a birthday cake cookbook. Every year, Annabelle spent ages choosing which one she wanted her mum to make.

For the winter party she chose the penguin cake. Annabelle's mum put blue jelly around the outside so it looked like the penguin was floating on water. When Annabelle had a farm party, her mum made a pink pig cake. She also made a batch of cupcakes and decorated them so that they looked like pigs' snouts. Everyone got their own snout to take home!

But this year Annabelle didn't want the same old party food. So at lunchtime she looked up the Party Princess site again.

THE PARTY PRINCESS SUGGESTS
- *Nori rolls*
- *Fried wontons*
- *Olives*
- *Blue cheese on mini-toast*
- *Spinach and cheese triangles*

Annabelle didn't know if she liked all of these things. *But the Party Princess is a party expert*, thought Annabelle. So she wrote all her suggestions down.

'OK, Belly,' said her mum, when Annabelle got in the car after school. 'What do we need?'

Annabelle read out her list. Her mum raised an eyebrow. 'Are you sure you want these things?' she said. 'I thought you hated olives.'

'I used to when I was little. But I'm sure I'll like them now,' said Annabelle quickly. 'And I really like nori rolls. I have them at Michiko's house all the time.'

'Maybe we can ask Michiko's mum to

help us make them?' suggested Annabelle's mum. 'And we can make the spinach and cheese triangles ourselves.'

Annabelle nodded. She liked cooking.

They parked near the bakery. In the window was a cake just like the one Nicole had at her party. Annabelle pressed her nose against the window.

I wish I could have a cake like that, she thought. But she knew her mum really liked making her birthday cakes. *I won't say anything,* decided Annabelle.

But somehow the words just blurted out anyway.

'Mum, could I have a cake from the shop this year?'

Annabelle's mum looked in the bakery window.

'Those cakes cost lots of money, Bell.'

'I know. But I want one *so* much!' said Annabelle. Then she had an idea. 'The cake can be my birthday present!' she said.

Her mum laughed.

'You don't really want a cake for a present, do you?' she said.

Annabelle nodded her head really hard and jumped up and down on the spot.

'Yes, I really, really do!'

'OK, OK!' laughed her mum. 'Let's go in and order one.'

Chapter Six

The days leading up to Annabelle's party seemed to go very slowly. It was lucky that she had to practise for the concert. This kept her busy, at least.

Then one morning Annabelle woke up with a fluttery feeling in her stomach. *Why am I excited?* she wondered. And then she remembered. *That's right, it's my birthday!*

She was a year older than when she

went to bed. How weird! Annabelle lay there for a moment, trying to tell if she felt different.

She wiggled her toes. They felt the same. Then she looked at her hands. They looked exactly the same too.

But I do feel a bit different, Annabelle decided. *Like I'm a bit taller. But just on the inside, so no-one else would notice.*

Annabelle's mum came into her room, carrying a tray.

'Happy birthday, Belly!' she said, putting the tray down on the bed.

Annabelle always had breakfast in bed on her birthday.

'Yum!' said Annabelle.

It was her favourite – French toast with banana and maple syrup, and a glass of chocolate milk.

'Don't stay in bed too long,' said her mum. 'There are lots of things to do.'

Just as Annabelle finished eating, the doorbell rang.

'I'll get it!' said Annabelle, jumping up.

She was too excited to stay in bed any-way.

She opened the door. A lady was standing there, holding a pink and gold box.

'Cake for Miss Bowan,' said the lady, smiling.

'That's me!' said Annabelle, and the lady handed her the box.

Annabelle carried it carefully to the kitchen. Her mum was there, stirring a bowl full of green and white gunky stuff.

'What's that?' asked Annabelle, wrinkling her nose.

'This is the spinach and cheese mixture for the triangles,' said her mum. 'They were on your list, remember? Have you changed your mind?'

'No, no,' replied Annabelle quickly. 'I just didn't think they'd be so icky-looking.'

'They won't look icky when they're cooked,' said her mum.

Annabelle helped her mum wrap the mixture up in strips of filo pastry. Then they put them in the oven. When the first batch came out they smelt great. And they didn't look icky at all!

Then Annabelle thought of something.

She turned to her mum.

'What should we serve them on?'

The Party Princess had said the food should be served on silver platters. But Annabelle was pretty sure they didn't have any of those.

'What about these?' said her mum, smiling.

To Annabelle's surprise she was holding two large silver platters.

'They used to belong to your grandma,' explained her mum. 'They've been hiding in the cupboard for years. I think this is the perfect chance to use them again.'

The platters looked a bit old. But Annabelle's mum found some silver polish and

Annabelle scrubbed them until they shone. She had just finished when Michiko's mum, Mrs Takasaka, arrived.

Mrs Takasaka put a bamboo mat on the table. Then she got out a bag of what looked like dark green paper squares.

'This is the nori,' explained Mrs Takasaka. 'You lay it on the bamboo mat. Next you put a layer of rice on top and squash it down flat. Then you put a line of your favourite fillings in the middle. Finally, you roll it all up and cut it into pieces.'

It looked really easy when Mrs Takasaka did it. But when Annabelle tried, it wouldn't stay rolled up. And all the filling came squishing out the ends.

'Too big, maybe,' said Mrs Takasaka.

So Annabelle tried again with less filling. This time the rolls stayed together. Mrs Takasaka chopped them into discs with a very sharp knife.

'Wow!' said Annabelle. 'They look just like shop ones.'

Mrs Takasaka laughed.

'Try one. I bet ours are much tastier.'

Annabelle picked one up. She loved nori rolls. And these ones looked really good.

'Mrs Takasaka,' she said, as she munched on one, 'what is nori exactly?'

'It's a type of seaweed,' replied Mrs Takasaka.

Annabelle stared at Mrs Takasaka in

horror. Mrs Takasaka laughed when she saw Annabelle's face.

Annabelle's mum came over.

'Belly! Look at the clock!' she said. 'You'd better get ready. Your friends will be arriving soon. We'll finish up in here.'

Annabelle hurried to her bedroom. She got her blue V-neck top out of the chest of drawers, and pulled on her skirt with the beaded waistband. It was her favourite outfit. But it was the sort of thing she always wore to parties.

I need something different for this party, decided Annabelle.

She opened up her wardrobe. At first nothing looked quite right. But then she saw her new concert clothes hanging right at the back.

She felt the edge of the skirt. The material made a nice *shushing* noise between her fingers.

'I'm sure Mum won't mind if I wear

this outfit today,' Annabelle told herself. 'It's my birthday, after all!'

Then she quickly got dressed.

Just as she finished doing her hair the doorbell rang. Annabelle looked in the mirror. It was already a hot day and her new clothes were quite warm. And she would have to be careful to keep them clean. But Annabelle didn't care.

It was absolutely the most perfect outfit for a mocktail party.

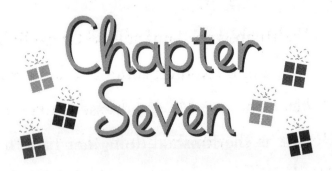

Chapter Seven

Annabelle ran to the front door. It was
Uncle Bob and Sophie. Sophie was wearing
a black skirt with sequins and a red satin
top. It was funny to see Sophie dressed up
because she usually just wore jeans. Today
she was even wearing a necklace!

'Cool outfit, Soph!' said Annabelle.

'Thanks,' said Sophie. 'I borrowed this
stuff from my friend Megan.'

'What about *my* outfit?' said Uncle Bob.

Annabelle looked at him and laughed. Uncle Bob was dressed up in a tuxedo. He was even wearing a bow tie.

'You look great, too,' said Annabelle, giving him a big kiss.

Sophie handed Annabelle a parcel.

'Happy birthday!' she said.

Annabelle opened it immediately.

Inside was a double picture frame decorated with beads and shells. In one frame was a drawing of Annabelle. In the other was one of Sophie. Annabelle was poking her tongue out at Sophie. And Sophie was poking hers out at Annabelle.

Annabelle laughed.

This was how she and Sophie sometimes said hello to each other.

'I decorated the frame,' explained Sophie.

'And she did the drawings, too,' added Uncle Bob.

Annabelle went and put it on her bedside table. Then she hugged Sophie.

'I love it so much! Thank you.'

The doorbell rang again. This time it was Chloe, Dani, Lola and Sarah. They were all wearing long, bright dresses and lots of crazy jewellery.

'Hi, guys!' she said. 'Where's Nic?' Then she felt a pang as she remembered. 'Oh yeah, that's right. She's coming later.'

For a moment, Annabelle felt a bit sad. It would be nice if Nicole was already here. But it was hard to be sad for long with her second besties around.

'Happy birthday!' they yelled excitedly, and gave Annabelle her presents.

Chloe gave her a CD and some stickers. Dani gave her a diary. Sarah and Lola gave her some green bracelets and matching hairclips.

'Thanks!' said Annabelle. 'Hey, you guys look really tall!'

Her friends grinned and lifted up their hems. They were all wobbling on shoes that were way too big.

'We borrowed my sister's stuff,'

explained Dani. 'I don't know how she could wear these shoes. They are sooo uncomfortable!'

Next to arrive were some other girls from their class. Then came Michiko and Shae. The last guests to turn up were Siri and Freya. Annabelle looked around at her friends. She almost didn't recognise them in their mocktail outfits.

'Wow, you all look so fantastic!' she grinned.

Then Uncle Bob appeared around the corner, carrying a silver tray. Balanced on top were glasses filled with brightly coloured soft drinks. Some drinks were red and pink. Some were green and blue.

A few were rainbow-striped. Each glass had a bendy straw, and some even had little umbrellas.

'Cooooool!' said everyone together.

Chloe had trouble choosing a drink.

'I don't know which one to have!' she said. 'They all look so good.'

'Don't worry, madam,' said Uncle Bob in a funny voice. 'I will be back with more.'

Chloe giggled as Uncle Bob left the room.

'The waiter called me madam!' she said.

'That's not a waiter,' laughed Annabelle. 'That's Uncle Bob!'

She tried her mocktail. It was delicious.

Then Annabelle's mum came in with

a tray of food in each hand. She raised an eyebrow when she saw that Annabelle was wearing her special concert clothes. Annabelle went red. She had a bad feeling her mum might make her get changed.

But all her mum said was, 'Be careful in those, won't you?'

'Do you have any mini-pizzas, Julia?' Dani asked Annabelle's mum.

'I hope so,' added Sarah. 'Yours are the best!'

'We've got different food this year,' explained Annabelle's mum. 'These are spinach and cheese triangles.'

Dani and Sarah both looked at them doubtfully.

'I don't really like spinach,' said Sarah.

'Annabelle,' said Dani, 'you try one first.'

Annabelle picked one up.

The triangles looked nice on the outside. They were golden brown from the oven and smelt really good.

But she kept remembering the green goopy stuff inside.

I'll just pretend it tastes nice, thought Annabelle, taking a bite.

'What's it like?' asked Sarah.

'Actually, it's delicious!' said Annabelle, surprised.

Everyone grabbed one and started munching away. Then Annabelle's mum held out the tray of nori rolls.

'These were handmade by Annabelle!' she said.

'Yum!' said Siri. 'They're my favourite!'

Everyone took one straight away.

'I bet you guys don't know what nori is,' Annabelle said as she picked one up.

'Of course we do!' said Lola and Sophie at the same time.

'Seaweed!' said Sarah.

Everyone else knows it's seaweed!

Annabelle thought she must have been the only person in the world who didn't known what nori was! She watched her friends as they helped themselves to seconds and thirds.

It wasn't long before all the triangles and nori rolls had been eaten.

Everyone is enjoying themselves, Annabelle thought happily. *This is turning out to be a great party!*

But then, quite suddenly, everything changed.

Chapter Eight

Uncle Bob came around with another tray of mocktails. Annabelle chose a rainbow one and took a big sip. This one didn't taste quite as nice as the first one. It tasted really, really sweet. Usually Annabelle loved sweet things. But this was a bit too sweet even for her.

Then she looked around at her friends. *Are they getting bored?* worried Annabelle.

I'd better put some music on!

She jumped up and went to the CD player. But what should she play?

I wish Nic was here to choose something, thought Annabelle.

Then she remembered the CD that Chloe had given her.

'Come on!' Annabelle said, as the CD came on. 'Let's dance!'

'Can we listen to something else?' complained Siri. 'I hate this CD!'

Chloe looked surprised.

'How can you hate it? It's the best!'

'I think it's dumb, too,' said Freya. 'And it's really hard to dance to.'

'It's too hot to dance anyway,' said Shae.

'Maybe we should swim instead?'

My friends are fighting! thought Anna-belle. This was exactly what she had been afraid of. She wished Nicole was here. She would know what to do.

Then Dani jumped up.

'It's easy to dance to this music,' she said. 'Just watch.'

She started doing a really funny dance.

She waved her arms around and jumped all over the place. It was so silly that everyone started laughing. And before long everyone else was dancing, too. Even Siri and Freya.

After a few songs, Dani flopped onto the couch.

'I have to stop dancing,' she said. 'I think those mocktails are turning into milkshakes in my tummy!'

'Same!' said Chloe, as she lay down on the floor.

It wasn't long before everyone else was lying down.

'My tummy keeps going *blurrrp!*' said Freya, laughing.

'Mine too!' said Lola. 'I can feel all that yummy food and too many mocktails sloshing around.'

Just then, Uncle Bob appeared.

'Would anyone like another mocktail?' he asked.

'NOOOO!' groaned everyone.

'Let's go outside,' said Sophie.

'We could play that game you told us about,' said Siri to Annabelle. 'Croaky?'

At first Annabelle wasn't sure what Siri meant. Then she realised Siri meant croquet. But Annabelle had forgotten to check what croquet was!

'Maybe we could play musical chairs instead?' she suggested.

Uncle Bob was still in the room, clearing away glasses.

'Ladies,' he said, bowing. 'Please follow me outside.'

Curiously, everyone followed him out the back door. The fresh air made Annabelle feel better straight away. Then she noticed something weird about the backyard. There were lots of little metal hoops sticking out of the ground! Leaning against the fence were wooden hammers with long handles.

'What's going on, Uncle Bob?' Annabelle whispered.

'It's a croquet set,' Uncle Bob replied. 'It's my present to you. I haven't played it for years. But I'm sure I can still remember the rules.'

'Thanks, Uncle Bob,' said Annabelle, hugging him. He was such a great uncle!

It turned out that croquet was a pretty fun game. The hammers were called mallets and you used them to hit a ball through the hoops. And Uncle Bob added a new rule. Every time you got the ball through a hoop you had to croak like a frog!

'I love this game!' said Freya.

'It's cool, isn't it?' agreed Chloe. 'But it'd be much easier without these dumb shoes on.'

They all kicked off their shoes and started playing in bare feet.

This is great! thought Annabelle happily.

Then all of a sudden Chloe screamed.

'OOOOWWWW!'

Annabelle's mum came running out of the house.

'What's happened?'

Annabelle could tell that Chloe was trying hard not to cry.

'My foot really, really hurts,' she said, with a wobbly voice.

Annabelle's mum quickly looked at Chloe's foot.

'It's a bee sting,' she said. 'You'd better sit inside and put your foot up. Everyone else wait here. It's time for the cake!'

Poor Chloe, thought Annabelle. *Bee stings really hurt!*

And to make things worse she was going to miss out on seeing the cake.

Chapter Nine

'Here it comes!' called Siri.

The back door opened and out came Uncle Bob, carrying the cake. It was decorated with candles and sparklers. Everyone sang Happy Birthday as Uncle Bob put the cake down on a fold-up table in front of Annabelle.

Usually Annabelle loved this part. But today it didn't feel quite right. It was like something was missing. Then Annabelle realised what it was.

Nicole still wasn't there!

Maybe she's decided not to come after all, thought Annabelle, disappointed.

When the singing stopped someone called out, 'Hip hip!'

'Hooray!' shouted everyone else.

'Hip hip!' said the voice again.

Annabelle looked around. It sounded like the voice was coming from over the fence. And then it was her turn to shout 'hooray', because coming through the back gate was Nicole!

Nicole was still wearing her basketball clothes. She was bright red in the face.

'Did you win?' asked Annabelle.

Nicole pulled a face.

'Well, actually ... ' she said.

Annabelle's heart sank. *Poor Nic! She must have lost. What a shame!*

But then Nicole's face broke into a smile. 'We won!'

'That's so great!' said Annabelle, jumping up and down.

'Is anyone going to blow out these candles?' asked Uncle Bob. 'The cake is going to catch on fire soon!'

'Oops!' said Annabelle.

She turned around and blew out all the candles in one breath.

'Don't forget to make a wish!' said

Chloe, who had hobbled back outside.

Annabelle shut her eyes and thought about what to wish for. Usually she wished for a pony.

But today she had a different wish.

I wish it could be my birthday forever!

Annabelle's mum handed her a knife with a pink ribbon tied around the handle. As Annabelle cut the cake she was careful not to touch the bottom so her wish would come true. Then her mum cut the cake into slices and handed them around.

Nicole took a bite of hers.

'Hey, this is like the cake I had at my party!' she said.

'It's from the same bakery,' explained Annabelle. 'It's so yum, isn't it?'

'It *is* yum,' agreed Nicole. 'But the ones your mum makes are even better.'

'Yeah,' said Michiko. 'Your mum's cakes rock. I love all the cool shapes and colours she makes them.'

'Me too,' said Lola. 'I always love your invitations, too. I've kept all of them!'

Annabelle stared at her friends. She

was too surprised to say anything. Did everyone like her old parties after all?

'I thought … ' she started to say.

But Annabelle didn't get to finish her sentence because suddenly Sophie yelled, 'Look out!'

Annabelle spun around.

The fold-up table the cake was sitting on was starting to collapse!

'Oh, no!' cried Annabelle.

She rushed forward to catch the cake before it fell. But before she got there she tripped on a rock and fell flat on her face.

A second later the cake toppled off the table. It fell with a splat beside her.

'Are you OK?' asked Michiko, helping
Annabelle up.

Annabelle looked down at her clothes.
There was a big grass stain on her shirt
and a rip in her skirt. And birthday cake
everywhere!

When Mum sees my concert clothes I'm going to be in big trouble, thought Annabelle, her eyes blurry with tears.

That was when Annabelle decided she'd had enough of this party. Everything was meant to be perfect on your birthday. But things just kept going wrong.

Annabelle ran into the house and into her bedroom. She got changed and then flopped down on her bed.

It was strange. Not long ago she had wished that her birthday would last forever. Now she just wanted it to be over.

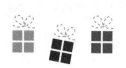

Chapter Ten

Annabelle's violin was in its case next to her bed. She picked it up. Playing music always made her feel better. But today it only helped a bit. Definitely not enough to want to go back outside.

After she had been playing for a while there was a knock on her door.

'Can I come in?' asked her mum.

Annabelle looked at her concert clothes

crumpled up on the floor. She didn't want
her mum to see that she had ruined them.
But there was no point hiding them. Her
mum would find out in the end.

'OK,' said Annabelle.

Her mum came in and sat beside her.

'You are playing so well, Belly,' she said.
'I can't wait to hear you at the concert.'

'I won't be able to play,' said Annabelle
sadly.

'Why not?' asked her mum, surprised.

'Because I've wrecked my concert clothes,' admitted Annabelle, showing her.

Annabelle's mum looked at the grass stain and the tear.

'You know, these aren't too bad. I think that grass stain will come out. And I can sew up that tear so you won't even know it's there. Besides,' she added. 'You have to play at the concert so you can wear this.'

She handed Annabelle a small blue box with a purple ribbon tied around it.

Annabelle was confused.

'But I thought the cake was my present,' she said.

'This isn't really a birthday present,'

explained her mum. 'It's to show how proud I am that you're about to play in your first concert.'

Annabelle opened the box.

Inside was a small silver treble clef, hanging on a chain.

'It's so beautiful!' said Annabelle. 'Can I wear it today or do I have to wait for the concert?'

'You can wear it today,' her mum laughed. 'Put it on and then come with me. There's something else you should see.'

Annabelle followed her mum into the kitchen. All her friends were crowded around the kitchen table.

'What's going on?' asked Annabelle.

Her friends all stepped to the side. Annabelle couldn't believe it. There on the table was a brand new birthday cake! It was shaped like a castle with lots of pointy turrets.

'Do you like it?' asked Nicole. 'We made

it out of ice-cream! And the turrets are ice-cream cones.'

'Yeah, what do you think?' said Chloe. 'Is it as good as the other one?'

Annabelle looked at the cake. It was already starting to melt. On the side some-one had written, 'Happy Birthday, Bell!' in chocolate dots. Some of the letters were much bigger than the others.

Annabelle looked at her friends.

'Are you kidding?' she said. 'It's *way* better than the other one!'

'Hey!' said Nicole. 'This means we can sing Happy Birthday again. But let's sing it the other way this time.'

As she started singing, everyone else

joined in. Even Annabelle's mum!

Happy birthday to you

You live in the zoo

You look like a monkey

And you smell like one too!

When the song finished, everyone cheered again. And this time it was even louder than before.

'Let's eat the cake!' said Annabelle.

Then she grabbed one of the turret-cones and used it to scoop up some of the ice-cream castle.

'Cool!' giggled Sarah, reaching out for a turret.

Before long everyone else was licking a turret, too.

'How about a swim?' suggested Lola.

'Great idea,' agreed Sophie, starting to head outside. Then she stopped. 'Hang on … None of us have our bathers.'

'Wait there!' said Annabelle, dashing out of the room.

She ran to her bedroom and grabbed as many T-shirts as she could find. Five minutes later, everyone was in the pool. Annabelle couldn't stop laughing. It was so funny to see everyone swimming around in her clothes.

Nicole swam up to her.

'I wish I'd been here from the start,' she said. 'Everyone keeps telling me what a great party it's been.'

Annabelle was surprised. She hadn't thought the party was very good at all. But then she thought about the day. A few bad things had happened. Like Chloe getting a bee sting. And the cake getting wrecked. But there had been lots of good things, too.

She looked around at everyone playing in the pool. Sophie and Michiko were both trying to sit on the li-lo, but they kept falling off. Dani was teaching the others her crazy dance. It looked even crazier in the water.

'I guess it *has* been pretty good,' said Annabelle, smiling. 'But I wonder what the Party Princess would say about it?'

'Who cares what *she* thinks?' Nicole sang out. 'You know more about parties than she does, any day!'

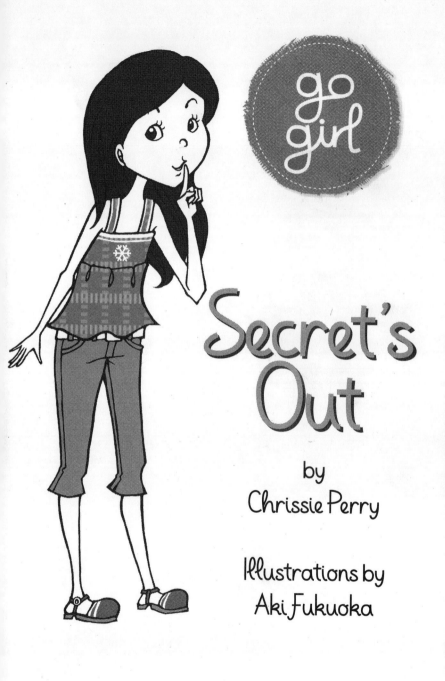

go girl

Secret's
Out

by
Chrissie Perry

Illustrations by
Aki Fukuoka

Chapter One

The hallway was noisy and busy, like it always was on Friday afternoons. It looked like a crazy jumble of arms and legs. Everyone seemed to be in a big rush to start the weekend.

Casey ducked in next to Tamsin and tugged her schoolbag down from its peg.

'Have you got everything?' Casey asked.

Tamsin nodded happily. Her parents were going away for the weekend, and so she was staying with Casey.

'I've got my pyjamas, my toothbrush ... and my dookie,' Tamsin giggled.

Casey smiled back. Tamsin was funny about her dookie. At Nina's birthday sleep-over, Tamsin had taken a piece of red velvet to bed with her and rubbed it against her nose as she fell asleep.

It was one of those things Casey would have been embarrassed about. But the good thing about Tamsin was that she totally didn't care if her friends knew.

'Look what else I've got,' Tamsin whispered. 'A midnight snack.'

Out of her bag, from underneath the pyjamas, came a giant bag of mixed lollies.

'Oh, not fair!' Ivy exclaimed from across the hall. She screwed up her nose. 'I wish I could come!'

Casey smiled at her apologetically. 'Sorry, Ives,' she said. 'I really did try, but Mum said that one extra person for two nights was enough.'

Casey and Tamsin quickly ducked as a very mouldy apple flew past them.

'It's a goal!' yelled Dylan Moltby, throwing his arms in the air as the apple landed in the rubbish bin.

'Ewww!' Tamsin groaned. 'How long was *that* in your bag?'

Dylan grinned. 'Months, I think. Maybe years,' he said proudly.

Casey hid her grin as Dylan ran off.

'So, are you guys going to eat *all* of those lollies by yourselves?' asked Nina, who was now standing beside the girls, looking at the lolly packet. 'Or would you be kind enough to save some red snakes for me?'

'And will you save me some yellows?' Ivy added. 'Pretty please?'

'Red and yellow snakes will be totally untouched and ready for you guys,' Tamsin declared with a smile.

Casey waved goodbye as Ivy and Nina walked off. As she looked across at Tamsin, Casey felt a little shiver of excitement.

Casey wouldn't have said anything, but she was sort of glad she wasn't allowed to have Ivy and Nina over as well.

Even though Tamsin wasn't really new at their school anymore, it was still exciting to be around her.

At the beginning, everybody had wanted to hang out with Tamsin – except for Casey. It had been kind of hard watching a new girl march right into her group of friends, so Casey hadn't been very nice to Tamsin.

Maybe she would have handled it better if things had been OK at home. But Tamsin had arrived at school when Casey's parents were fighting a lot.

Casey had felt like everything in her life was changing, and all she wanted was for things to stay the same.

Casey felt a bit bad as she remembered how she had totally ignored Tamsin. Ivy and Nina were friendlier, and had got to know Tamsin really quickly.

After a while, Casey had realised that Tamsin was funny and nice. But there were still lots of things she didn't know about her, even though now they were in a club together with Nina and Ivy. The club was called the Secret Sisters.

It was completely different with Ivy and Nina. Casey had known those girls since they were all little. She knew them inside out. She knew their favourite colours and their favourite food, their favourite books and their favourite music.

'Oh, I brought my Taylor Swift CD,' Tamsin said, interrupting Casey's thoughts. She was fishing around in her schoolbag again. 'Do you like her, Case?'

Casey nodded. She'd just been thinking about music, and it was almost like Tamsin had read her mind. And Taylor Swift was, like, her second-favourite singer ever!

Casey grinned to herself as she and Tamsin walked down the corridor together and out into the warm afternoon sunshine. She giggled as Tamsin tossed the lolly bag into the air and caught it behind her back.

This weekend is going to be so fun, Casey thought happily. By Sunday, she and Tamsin would know everything about each other.

Then Casey's tummy did a funny little flip. *Maybe,* she thought, *just maybe, I'll even tell Tamsin my special secret.*

Chapter Two

'Let's turn it up again,' Casey said, reaching for the volume on the CD player.

Tamsin put her hands over her ears. Between the girls' music and the thumping rock tunes coming from Aaron's bedroom, the noise was pretty full-on.

'Turn it down!' The door to Casey's bedroom swung open, and her brother stomped inside.

'Hey, you can't do that!' Casey yelled.

But Aaron had already pushed the pause button.

'You are such a dweeb!' Casey said. 'You get to play your music all the time.'

'Yeah, but *my* music is good!' Aaron said. He stood between Casey and the CD player, his arms folded.

'Hang on, so is ours,' Tamsin piped up. 'How about *we* get half an hour of our music, and then you can have half an hour of yours?'

Casey looked from Tamsin to Aaron. To Casey's surprise, Aaron seemed to be considering the deal.

'Ummm . . . nup,' he said finally.

'Then how about we get a whole hour, and we do something for you?' Tamsin went on. 'One of your jobs, maybe?'

'Yeah, like we'll set the table for you tonight,' Casey said.

Aaron looked as though he was weakening. '*And* I get to choose what TV we watch after dinner,' he bargained.

'OK,' Casey and Tamsin chimed in together.

Aaron walked out, looking very smug and satisfied.

'Hey, good work!' Casey whispered. 'Especially since it was *my* turn to set the table tonight!'

Tamsin burst out laughing. 'Brothers!'

Casey shook her head as she turned the CD player back on. It was great fun to dance around her bedroom with Tamsin. It was even better to find someone who knew what it was like to have a big brother.

Ivy had a sister and Nina was an only child. They didn't know anything about brothers. But Tamsin totally understood.

It looked like she and Tamsin had even more in common than Casey had hoped.

'Can you believe the noise Aaron made with his pappadums?' Casey said in bed that night, pulling her doona up under her chin.

'He was truly disgusting,' Tamsin giggled. 'But not quite as disgusting as Julian. My brother actually *drinks* his peas! He puts them on his tongue, gets a glass of water and swallows them down whole. It's gross.'

Casey turned onto her tummy and looked down at Tamsin, who was lying on the trundle bed.

It's so nice having a friend sleep over, thought Casey. Especially a friend who understood her life so well.

'Would you swap Aaron for a big sister?' Tamsin asked, stifling a big yawn.

Casey thought for a moment. It was a good question. Aaron could be a real pain. But then again, when she was having trouble with her maths homework, Aaron was the one who always helped her work out the problems.

And they had the best fun doing Warrior Wrestling matches. They made up silly names like Buster Strong-Heart and Lady Muck … and Lady Muck was getting pretty good at getting Buster into a headlock!

'No,' Casey said finally. 'I actually wouldn't swap.'

Tamsin sighed sleepily. 'Me neither,' she said softly.

Casey put her arms behind her head and stared up at the ceiling. She felt really close to Tamsin at the moment. She felt like she could really talk to her.

Casey took a deep breath. Tamsin was definitely the right person to tell her special secret to.

It was something she hadn't told a single person, and it had been sitting inside her for at least two weeks!

'Tam?' she whispered, leaning over the side of the bed.

But Tamsin didn't say anything. Casey smiled to herself when she caught sight of the dookie lying on the pillow beside Tamsin's head.

Oh well, she thought, snuggling back under her doona. *Luckily we've got the whole weekend together. I can tell her tomorrow.*

Chapter Three

Casey normally got dragged to watch Aaron's soccer games on Saturday mornings. She would sit in the car for a while doing the kids' crossword in the newspaper. Then she would get a hot dog. Then she would wait a bit longer before getting a lemonade.

The idea was to stretch out everything good about going to soccer for as long as she could. But even with this plan, Saturday mornings were usually pretty boring.

Today was different, though. Casey and Tamsin were having the best fun in the playground next to the soccer field, mucking around in the old boat.

'OK, let's make it that I've got the treasure and you have to try and tap my shoulder three times before I hand it over,' Casey suggested.

'Yeah,' Tamsin agreed. 'And let's . . .' she trailed off, looking over Casey's shoulder at something. 'Hey!' called Tamsin, giving a little wave.

Casey looked in the direction of the wave. Ben Maddison, who went to their school, was walking over to them. He was staring at his feet as though his runners were the most interesting thing in the world. In fact, he hardly glanced up until he arrived at the boat.

'Hey, Ben. Are you watching someone play?' Tamsin asked.

Ben nodded, inspecting the boat's flaking paint. 'My brother,' he mumbled.

'Oh, which one is he?' said Tamsin.

Ben pointed awkwardly at a tall, lanky boy on the field.

Casey sat back in the boat and watched as Tamsin chatted to Ben. Tamsin was good at it, and she didn't seem to get shy. After a minute, Ben seemed less shy, too.

In fact, Casey noticed with a smile, soon Ben and Tamsin were laughing at one of the soccer players who'd taken a major dive in the dirt.

Eventually, Ben said goodbye and jogged back to the soccer field.

'He's cute, don't you think?' Tamsin asked thoughtfully. 'I think I might like him a bit, you know?'

'Really?' Casey asked.

Suddenly, her heart was thumping. Tamsin had told her something pretty special. And even though Casey had planned on telling Tamsin her own secret later on that night, before they went to sleep, it felt like now was the right time.

'Ah, Tamsin?' she said, but she sounded a bit croaky. She cleared her throat. 'Ah, Tamsin?' she repeated.

'Yeah?'

'I, er … I like Dylan Moltby.'

It felt strange to say it out loud. That secret had been stuck inside her for ages.

Casey had kept it totally to herself while Dylan stood around at lunchtime, telling jokes that made everyone laugh. And she kept it to herself when she sat behind Dylan in assembly.

Casey hadn't told anyone. Not Ivy. Not Nina. Not *anyone*.

So Casey had imagined Tamsin's jaw dropping in surprise when she told her. But it wasn't quite like that.

'Oh, yeah,' Tamsin said, nodding. 'Dylan Moltby is really nice. I mean, he's funny and stuff.'

Suddenly, Tamsin got a sneaky look on her face. She reached over and swatted Casey's shoulder three times.

'Hand over the treasure!' she demanded with a giggle.

Casey tried to duck, but it was too late. 'Hey,' she laughed. 'I wasn't ready!'

Tamsin had already scrambled away with the imaginary treasure.

'All right,' Casey yelled. 'I am *so* going to get you!'

The rest of the day was just as much fun as the start. But it went way too quickly, not like an ordinary weekend at all.

That night, the girls turned the lights off and climbed into bed. It was kind of naughty to clean your teeth, and then go to bed with a giant packet of lollies!

'Don't rustle the packet too much or Mum will come in,' Casey warned.

Tamsin grinned at her. 'Turn on the torch so I can see what I'm doing,' Tamsin whispered, popping another lolly in her mouth.

Casey turned the torch on, and Tamsin tipped all the lollies out of the bag. She carefully separated the red and yellow snakes, and put them into a little plastic bag they'd pinched out of the kitchen drawers.

'Do you think Ivy and Nina would know if we just ate one each?' Tamsin asked cheekily.

Casey shook her head. 'Not if we don't tell them,' she whispered.

After they'd eaten lots of lollies, Casey's

teeth felt all sugary. She thought about getting up and brushing them, but her eyelids felt heavy and tired.

Casey looked down at Tamsin in the torchlight, and saw her nicking another red snake. There weren't that many left in the bag, actually. If Casey had the energy, she would have told Tamsin to stop.

But another part of her didn't mind.

Casey could keep a secret.

And so could Tamsin. Couldn't she?

Chapter Four

Going to school on a Monday could be hard. But coming back on a Monday to an Italian-themed lunch was excellent! Casey loved it when school was like this.

Mrs Massola, their Italian teacher, had done a really good job. There was a big trestle table set up in the playground. Steam rose up into the air from huge pots filled with pasta and bolognaise sauce.

Casey waved at her friends from behind the trestle table. She'd been chosen to help serve the food.

'OK, guys,' said Mrs Massola, 'when everybody lines up, you put a serve of pasta like this, and then a scoop of sauce.'

The first kids in line were Holly and Olivia from Mr Mack's class. Casey grinned and chatted as she scooped pasta into their bowls. She was having fun serving up. Even though her mouth was watering and she would have to wait until the end to eat!

Soon, the line was really long. It seemed to Casey that there were a gazillion mouths to feed. She had to speed up. After a while, she barely noticed who she was serving.

Until Dylan Moltby was standing in front of her. Suddenly, Casey's hands felt a little bit shaky. She got the pasta in the bowl, but only half of the sauce made it onto the pasta. The rest landed on the ground.

Casey grabbed a fresh bowl, her face burning, and started all over again.

Casey was sort of glad when Dylan took his bowl of pasta and walked off. She felt like her face was as red as the pasta sauce!

Next in line were her besties. Casey grinned at them.

'Hey, can I have heaps of pasta and just a little bit of sauce?' Nina asked.

'And I'll just have a giant helping of everything,' Ivy added. 'Like the serve you gave *Dylan*.'

Casey froze. Then she stared at her friends. She saw Tamsin give Ivy a little nudge in the ribs.

It was so *obvious*. Casey dropped the ladle into the pot, and glared at Tamsin.

Tamsin had *told*. Casey's secret was out!

After Casey had finished serving up the pasta, she took her bowl and marched over to the courtyard, away from everybody. She was furious.

She sat down, watching the cloud of steam as it drifted up from her bowl. For a moment, Casey imagined that the steam was coming from her ears, like it does in cartoons when someone is cross.

Everyone else had finished eating, but suddenly Casey didn't feel hungry at all.

She could hear the little kids squealing from the playground. She could hear a ball thumping along the court. They were the sounds of a regular lunchtime. But it didn't feel regular to Casey.

'Hey, Casey. Are you OK?' said a voice.

Casey looked up as Tamsin sat down beside her.

Nina and Ivy stood in front of them.

'I can't believe you told my secret,' Casey said, looking at her shoes.

'That you like Dylan?' asked Tamsin.

'Um, yeah.'

Casey turned and glared at Tamsin.

Tamsin shrugged. 'Oops,' she said, like it was no big deal. 'I didn't mean to do anything wrong. It's just that we were all talking about boys we like, and ... well ...' she trailed off.

'Hey, you guys,' called Ching Ching from across the courtyard. 'The littlies want us to play chasey with them. Who's in?'

She pointed to a bunch of little kids who had their hands together, begging the older girls to join their game.

'That could be fun,' Tamsin said softly, looking at Casey.

Casey crossed her arms tightly. It was *so* annoying the way Tamsin just expected everything to go back to normal.

Casey felt a wave of anger rushing through her. Before she had a chance to think, she opened her mouth and let it all pour out.

'Yeah, you *should* play with the babies,' she said furiously. 'Since you're a baby yourself with that stupid dookie you have to rub against your nose to get to sleep.'

Suddenly, everything went quiet.

Chapter Five

'That,' said Ivy, with her hands on her hips, 'was really, really mean, Casey!'

Casey stared down at her bowl of cold spaghetti bolognaise. She pushed it around with her plastic fork.

She could hear Ching Ching and Holly chasing the little kids. She could hear lots of giggling as they caught a little girl with long plaits. And she could hear Tamsin clearing her throat, as though she was trying not to cry.

Now that those terrible words had come out of her mouth, Casey had absolutely nothing left to say.

'Hang on,' said Nina, 'maybe Casey *was* a bit mean there. But Tamsin was pretty mean, too. If someone tells you a secret, you're not supposed to tell other people.'

'But Casey liking Dylan isn't really a secret,' Ivy protested. 'You all know who I like, and that's not such a big deal, is it?'

'No,' Nina said, 'but you don't *mind* that everyone knows who you like. If Casey didn't want anyone to know who she likes, then Tamsin shouldn't have told! And stop rolling your eyes, Ivy. It's really rude!'

It was like a ping-pong game, but with words instead of a little white ball. Ivy kept sticking up for Tamsin. Nina kept sticking up for Casey.

It was seriously weird how Tamsin hadn't said a word, and neither had Casey.

Casey sneaked a look at Tamsin. But Tamsin's head seemed to be stuck in her hands, and she didn't look up.

Suddenly Ivy grabbed Tamsin's hand and pulled her up to standing. 'Come on, Tamsin,' she said. 'Let's go and play by *ourselves*.'

The rest of the day was awful. Every time Casey thought about what she'd said to Tamsin, she felt sick to her stomach.

Whenever Casey tried to steal a glance at Tamsin, Tamsin would look away.

Whenever she tried to look at Ivy, Ivy stared back with her eyebrows raised.

During maths class, the problems on the sheet seemed impossible. Casey wasn't sure whether to add, subtract, multiply or divide.

I can't believe I said that to Tamsin.

Later, when they were supposed to be writing a diary entry about the Italian lunch, Casey's page stayed completely blank. She kept on imagining how good it would be if she could just write down the horrible thing she had said in pencil, and then rub it out. As though she could totally erase what she'd said from everybody's memory.

'Come on, Casey, get writing,' Mrs Withers said, standing behind her.

Casey nodded. She put her pencil to the page and started writing. Mrs Withers was right. She just had to get on with it.

Casey wrote about what it was like to serve out all that food. She wrote about the long queue, and chatting with Holly and Olivia. She even wrote about spilling Dylan's bolognaise sauce on the ground.

But as she was writing, Casey was thinking more about the things that she was leaving out of her diary entry than the things she was putting in there.

There was no way she could write about what had happened with Tamsin after she'd finished serving. It was confusing enough just thinking about it.

It was so upsetting that Tamsin had told the others her secret. A part of Casey still felt cross about it. But she also felt cross with herself. Really, really cross. She hadn't even meant to say that horrible thing to Tamsin. She actually thought Tamsin's dookie was kind of cute.

Casey felt like she and her friends were on a kind of see-saw. On one side, there was Tamsin telling everyone Casey's secret. On the other side, there was Casey being mean to Tamsin. And it was like Ivy had jumped onto Tamsin's end, and Nina had jumped onto Casey's.

Casey bit her lip. *How are we ever going to get off this see-saw?*

Chapter Six

'Hey, Case, how about some old-fashioned popcorn?' her mum asked, when Casey walked into the kitchen after school.

'What do you mean?' asked Casey quietly, taking the school newsletter out of her bag and putting it on the bench.

'You know, the kind that you make with oil in a saucepan, not in the microwave,' her mum said, raising an eyebrow. 'The kind you love, remember? Want some?'

Casey shrugged. 'I don't know.'

She sat on one of the bar stools on the other side of the counter. There was a lever underneath the seat that made it go up and down. Casey pulled it. She went up and down, up and down.

'You don't know whether you want *popcorn?*' her mum asked. She leant over the kitchen bench and put her hand on Casey's forehead.

'No fever,' her mum joked. 'So, what else could put my lovely daughter off popcorn?'

Casey could tell that her mum was waiting for her to crack a smile. But Casey just didn't feel like there was a smile inside her at the moment.

Her mum came around and sat on the bar stool next to Casey. She slyly reached under the stool for the lever, and started going up and down. But her timing was pretty bad.

When Casey rose up, her mum went down. When Casey went down, her mum rose up.

Actually, it was pretty funny. Casey tried hard not to smile, but in the end, after about twenty ups and downs, she couldn't help it.

'Hey, that's better,' her mum said. 'Can we please stop now? I'm getting dizzy.'

Finally, Casey and her mum were level with each other.

'What's wrong, sweetie?' her mum asked. This time, there was no joke in her voice. She sounded concerned.

'I had a really bad day.' Casey's voice crumbled as she spoke. But once she'd started, everything that had happened just tumbled out of her mouth.

She told her mum about liking Dylan. She told her mum about Tamsin telling everyone her secret. Then, and this was the hardest bit, she told her mum what she'd said to Tamsin about her dookie.

Casey's mum listened carefully.

'So, now,' Casey finished, 'I don't know what to do. Like, who's right and who's wrong?'

Casey's mum looked thoughtful. 'Maybe you're both right, and you're both wrong,' she said.

It was nice, sitting next to her mum, just talking.

'I was really upset when I found out that Tamsin had told the others about Dylan,' said Casey. 'I really just wanted it to be private. Don't you think it was mean for her to tell?'

'Did you ask Tamsin to keep it a secret?' her mum asked.

'Well, maybe not exactly,' Casey said. 'But it's obvious isn't it? Like, how am I supposed to be friends with someone I can't even trust?'

Casey's mum shook her head. 'Maybe it wasn't obvious to Tamsin,' she said. 'And you did trust all those girls when things were a bit rough here at home, didn't you? They were all pretty terrific then. Didn't they help you a lot, Case?'

Casey thought hard for a moment. Her mum was right. All of the Secret Sisters, Ivy, Nina, Tamsin and Casey, had taken turns helping each other.

Casey had to admit that they were the best friends when her mum and dad were fighting a lot. In fact, Casey wondered how she ever would have got through that time without them.

'I guess the thing is,' her mum went on, 'friends make mistakes. Even grown-up friends can make mistakes. Even parents make mistakes! Sometimes you have to try really hard to work things out.'

Casey nodded thoughtfully. And then she had an idea. Suddenly, Casey felt a little better. Actually, she felt absolutely starving.

'How about some of that old-fashioned popcorn, Mum?' she asked with a smile.

Chapter Seven

The next morning before school, Casey spent ages on the computer making pretty invitations. She put daisies all around the border, just like the daisies that decorated Tamsin's peg at school.

When she was finished, she printed out three invitations. Her heart fluttered as the pages came out of the printer.

TO THE SECRET SISTERS
You are invited to an
emergency meeting!
Place: Casey's cubby
Time: 4.30pm TODAY!

Aaron poked his head into the study.

'What are you doing up so early?' he asked, rubbing his eyes. 'And what are you printing? It woke me up, dweebarama.'

'Well, dweebarooma,' Casey replied, tucking the invitations into her schoolbag, 'I had something important to do.'

'Well, dweebarooni,' Aaron said, getting a little bag out of the pocket of his pyjamas and popping something red in his mouth, 'it was lucky you woke me up so early. You gave me heaps of time to find your stash!'

'Aaron!' Casey exclaimed. 'We were saving those for Nina and Ivy!'

Aaron grinned cheekily, popping a yellow snake in his mouth.

'Finders keepers!' he teased, waving the bag around. Then he narrowed his eyes. 'Unless,' he said dramatically, 'Lady Muck would like to wrestle me for the snakey prize?'

Casey rolled her eyes, but inside she was kind of glad. Warrior Wrestling was a great way to let off steam. And, even though she felt good about her plan to solve the argument between her friends, part of her still felt knotted up with worry about how the meeting would go.

Casey was already planning some good wrestling moves as she jogged out to the Warrior Wrestling trampoline.

Aaron beat her outside and jumped up to bounce-jog on the tramp, yelling in his loud commentator voice.

'Today, we have Lady Muck and Buster Strong-Heart fighting for the Red and Yellow Snakes Title,' he bellowed, using his hand as a microphone. 'Will Lady Muck be able to shake off last week's sad, bad performance to take the title? Or will Buster Strong-Heart be king yet again?'

Casey jumped up onto the trampoline, transforming herself into Lady Muck. She edged her way around the sides, doing little jumps and growling at Buster. He bounced around, punching the air with his fists.

Buster was pretty tricky. While Lady Muck was watching Buster's hands, Buster kicked out his leg, flipping Lady Muck behind the knees. Her legs buckled.

'And Lady Muck looks set to go down!' Buster yelled.

But Lady Muck recovered. She steadied her feet and rose up to standing position. She held her arm out and dived behind

Buster. And then Lady Muck sprung her famous headlock over his shoulder.

'One, two, three – ten!' she shouted. 'Lady Muck is the champion wrestler of the world. Hand over the loot, Buster Weak-Heart!'

Buster wriggled out of the headlock. Then he jumped off the trampoline and ran inside the house, giggling madly.

'Aaron!' Casey groaned. 'I won! And those lollies are for Ivy and Nina!'

Casey climbed off the tramp and followed her brother inside. She would have liked to dob on him, but she knew that Warrior Wrestling wasn't exactly popular with their parents, especially first thing on a school morning. Dobbing on Aaron would be dobbing on herself.

Casey rolled her eyes when she saw Aaron darting towards his bedroom.

She knew that once he went in there, there was absolutely no chance of her finding the lollies. Aaron's bedroom was like a rubbish tip!

Never mind, thought Casey, heading into the kitchen and pouring herself a bowl of cereal. *I've got more important things to worry about than red and yellow snakes. Like the emergency meeting at four-thirty this afternoon!*

Chapter Eight

That afternoon, Casey was pacing around her cubby house, looking at the photos on the wall. She paused in front of the one of her with Justin Bieber.

Tamsin's brother had cut and pasted pictures of the Secret Sisters with their very own star. If you looked closely you could tell the photos weren't real.

But Casey liked them anyway, and they made the cubby house look cool.

Casey sighed. She wanted things to go back to the way they were before.

School that day had been a bit better than yesterday. No-one had mentioned the argument, which was good, but also bad. Because even though the Secret Sisters had all played together with the girls from Mr Mack's class, it was obvious that something was still wrong.

Things weren't totally horrible any-more, but Casey felt like she and her best friends weren't as close as they had been before the argument. It used to feel like the four girls were linked together, like the links in a chain. Now, it felt like some of those links were about to snap.

I miss my friends.

Casey flopped into a beanbag. She picked up one of her favourite magazines and started flipping through the pages.

She caught sight of a picture of Taylor Swift, and remembered how she'd felt on Friday afternoon when Tamsin had asked if she liked her.

Casey sighed again. Friday afternoon seemed like a long time ago now.

Casey turned the page. In the centre spread, where staples held the magazine together, was a quiz called, *What sort of friend are you?*

Casey scanned the questions quickly. *Perhaps we can start the meeting by doing the friendship quiz together*, she thought, feeling a little happier. This was the sort of quiz they all loved. *Well, the sort of quiz we used to love . . .*

Casey's thoughts were interrupted by car doors slamming in her driveway.

Casey's tummy lurched a little as she peeked through the cubby house window. Ivy and Tamsin had arrived together!

It shouldn't have been such a surprise. Ivy and Tamsin lived in the same street, so it made sense for them to share a lift. Casey just felt a bit nervous that she would be there alone with them before Nina arrived.

'Hi, Tamsin! Hi, Ives!' Casey tried to keep her voice sounding bright. But it still wobbled a little bit.

Ivy walked through the cubby door in front of Tamsin, her arms crossed firmly.

'Well?' Ivy said.

Tamsin stood quietly next to Ivy.

Casey scratched her head. 'Well, what?'

'Well, you can say sorry to Tamsin now,' Ivy said bluntly.

Casey took a deep breath, and tried not to feel upset all over again.

'Hang on,' said Nina, suddenly appearing in the cubby house doorway. 'How about Tamsin says sorry first, since she's the one who did the wrong thing first?'

Nina walked over to Casey and stood next to her.

Casey closed her eyes. Nina and Ivy were at it all over again! This definitely wasn't working out the way she'd planned.

Tamsin took a sideways step, away from the protection of Ivy.

'I'm sorry, Casey,' Tamsin whispered.

For a moment, Casey wasn't sure whether she'd heard right over the noise of Ivy and Nina arguing. But then Tamsin continued.

'Case, I honestly didn't think . . . I still don't really understand why you liking Dylan was such a big secret. But I promise I didn't mean to betray your trust.'

Casey smiled weakly at Tamsin, and sat down in a beanbag. Tamsin flopped next to her, and Ivy and Nina sat opposite them. This time, Ivy and Nina didn't say anything. There was silence in the cubby house.

Casey bit her lip. She knew now that she had to make Tamsin understand why she had been so cross. It was a hard thing to explain, though. She just had to try to find the right words.

Casey stood up again and faced Tamsin. 'When I told you my secret,' she began slowly, 'it was like giving you a little piece of myself to take care of. I just thought . . . well, I expected you to understand that it was private.'

Casey paused for a moment while she thought about how to continue.

'I just think friends need to be able to trust each other with this kind of stuff,' she said eventually. 'I felt really sad and upset when you told the others, because it felt like you weren't looking after the piece of me that I'd given you.'

Casey stopped again, amazed that even the talkative Ivy was still quiet. She sat back down in the beanbag next to Tamsin.

Nina was nodding as though she understood. It definitely seemed as though everyone was really listening to what she had to say. And that felt good.

Casey felt a little worried she couldn't

see Tamsin's reaction, though. Tamsin was looking down at the floor.

'And besides,' Casey went on, 'I sort of freaked out that Dylan might find out. You know how when it gets out that you like someone, something changes between you? I really like Dylan as a friend. I don't want it to get all weird, like if he knows I like him . . . then we might act all goofy around each other.'

'Like getting all shaky when you're dishing out bolognaise sauce,' Ivy said with a little smile.

'Or walking straight into a pole when you're talking to someone in particular,' Nina added.

This time, Ivy and Nina both grinned. Ivy had whacked into a pole a week ago while she was talking to Adrian. Casey would have died of embarrassment if that had happened to her. But Ivy just thought it was funny, except for the bruise on her forehead!

Finally, Tamsin looked up. 'Yeah,' she said softly. 'That's true, I guess. It does get a bit strange when boys know you like them. But if you'd *explained* how you felt, I would have kept it a secret.' Tamsin's shoulders drooped a little. 'It was wrong of me to tell, though. I guess I made a mistake,' she finished quietly.

Casey bit her lip. Even though she was

glad they were talking, she was worried that Tamsin still looked unhappy.

And Casey knew deep down that there was something else she had to say to Tamsin. Because what Casey had done was way worse than making a mistake. She had deliberately tried to hurt Tamsin's feelings.

Casey had already forgiven Tamsin. But would Tamsin be able to forgive *her?*

Chapter Nine

Casey got up out of the beanbag and walked around the cubby. It felt as though there were so many words inside her that she had to stand up to give them more space.

'Tam,' she said, 'I, er, sometimes say things I don't mean when I'm angry.'

'That's true,' Ivy said. 'Like once, she told me I was never, ever going to be her —'

'*Everyone* says things they don't mean when they're angry,' Nina interrupted, giving Casey a supportive look, and Ivy a little pinch on the arm.

'Yeah, but maybe I'm a bit more like that than some people,' Casey admitted.

Casey noticed that Tamsin's eyebrows were raised, as though she wasn't quite sure what Casey was going to say next.

'When I said that thing about your dookie,' Casey said, 'I didn't actually mean it. I think your dookie is cute, Tam. And it was really, really mean of me to talk about it like that in front of everyone.'

Tamsin nodded, her face red. 'It *was* a bit embarrassing,' she said.

I just want to be friends again

Casey sat down next to Tamsin again. 'I'm super, super sorry,' she said, feeling like she might cry. She so badly wanted Tamsin to forgive her.

Tamsin looked Casey directly in the eye. Then she grabbed her hand. 'It's OK,' she said kindly. 'Everyone makes mistakes.'

Casey felt as though a great weight had been lifted off her shoulders. She smiled at Tamsin gratefully. 'Thanks . . .' she began.

But Tamsin and Ivy and Nina weren't looking at her anymore. They were looking over at the window.

Casey heard a dull thud on the glass. Then she saw one red and one yellow snake, hanging down from the top of the window frame. They were held by a familiar hand.

'I think your brother might be out on the roof,' Tamsin grinned.

'I think my brother might be out of his mind,' Casey groaned.

'Out of his mind and out on the roof, with *our* snakes!' Ivy squealed.

Suddenly, the Secret Sisters were all scrambling out the door. Casey giggled as Nina grabbed one of Aaron's legs, and Ivy grabbed the other.

Casey grinned to herself as the girls pulled Aaron down onto the balcony of the cubby house.

It was great to see everyone acting like they were on the same team again. It was even better to watch them win back the red and yellow snakes!

'Hey, you guys *did* save us the red and

yellow ones,' Ivy giggled as Aaron climbed down, chuckling.

Casey looked at Tamsin slyly.

Tamsin winked at her, and said cheekily, 'As if we wouldn't save them for you! What sort of friends do you think we are?'

Chapter Ten

Casey smiled as she poured each of her friends a glass of lemonade. It was fantastic to have everything back to normal.

'Hey, let's do that quiz,' Nina suggested, flipping through Casey's magazine. 'It's called, *What sort of friend are you?* Is everybody ready?'

'Yep!' the others called out together.

'All right, question one,' Nina began.

1. Do you know your friends'
   favourite colours, movies,
   singers, and actors?

'Definitely!' they all yelled.

Nina laughed as she put each of their initials next to the A on the quiz sheet. They spent so much time talking about this stuff there was no way any of them would get *that* question wrong.

Nina moved on to question two.

2. Have you been on camps
   or holidays together?

'Well, that's easy,' Ivy said. 'We all went on the school camp together last term. Remember how Casey freaked out on the flying fox? And her face was all screwed up like this?'

Everyone cracked up as Ivy did a great impression of Casey on the flying fox.

Hey, I wasn't that bad!

'Yeah, and I also remember a certain person falling over face first in the mud on the obstacle course,' Casey snorted.

It was ages until they got to question three. But nobody cared. It was just great fun doing the quiz together!

3. Do you include your friends in your birthday celebrations?

'Definitely,' Tamsin called out. Again, everybody agreed.

Nina was quiet for a moment as she studied the quiz page. Then she read out the next question.

4. Do you always tell the truth, even if it might hurt your friends' feelings?

'Yes,' Ivy said. 'Of course it's yes.'

Casey watched as Nina shook her head. 'No way, Ives,' she objected. 'Like, some things you just shouldn't say.'

'Yeah,' Tamsin agreed with Nina. 'For example, if Ivy got a new top that she absolutely loved, and I absolutely hated, I'm not going to tell her that, am I? That would just be mean.'

'But if she asked your opinion,' Casey said, 'then you should tell her the truth. Don't you think?'

'Of course you shouldn't!' Nina and Tamsin said together.

'Of course you should!' Ivy and Casey countered.

'Shouldn't!' Nina and Tamsin giggled.

'Should!' Casey and Ivy yelled.

'Shouldn't!'

Suddenly, all the girls were up, dancing around and singing 'should' and 'shouldn't'. Ivy was the first to put her 'should' into a funny little shimmy as she danced around the cubby.

Soon, though, all the Secret Sisters were shimmying to their own chant.

Casey paused for a minute, and watched her dancing, disagreeing friends.

It didn't matter that they had different opinions. Maybe they all had different rules for what they should tell and what they should keep secret.

Maybe they all had different ideas of when they should tell the truth, or when they should keep something to themselves.

And really, Casey was glad. The ideas that made them different also made each of them special.

Real life, and real friendships, weren't as simple as choosing an A or a B, like in a quiz.

And Casey wouldn't change that. Not for anything in the world.

go girl

Music
Mad

by
Rowan McAuley

Illustrations by
Aki Fukuoka

Chapter One

It was a warm day and the air conditioning in the car was broken. All the windows were down and a dusty wind blew everyone's hair into a tangle.

Iris didn't care one little bit. She was in the car on the way to her first music camp and nothing could put her in a bad mood. In the boot of the car, her saxophone was tuned and polished. She even had a brand new orange-and-purple sling for wearing around her neck while she played.

For four days and three nights she was going to be at Camp Melody. Imagine! Actually living with other kids who loved music as much as she did. Best of all, on the last day, they would perform in the concert – with their families watching.

'Iris?' called her mum from the driver's seat. 'Ask Kick if he needs to go to the toilet, would you? There's a service station up ahead, but we won't stop if we don't have to.'

Iris turned to her brother. He was reading a comic and had taken out his hearing aids because of the wind rushing through the car windows.

Iris tapped him on the arm. When he looked at her, she said, 'Mum says, do you need the toilet?'

He grinned. 'No, but I want a chocolate bar.'

'Hey, I heard that,' said their dad, looking up from reading the map.

Kick always spoke too loudly, even when he was trying to whisper.

'Dad heard that,' Iris repeated for him.

Kick shrugged. 'Well, I do!' He licked his lips. 'I want a huge chocolate bar with chocolate on the outside and chocolate fudge in the middle!'

'All right,' said their mum. 'I could do with some chocolate, too.'

'Mum says yes!' said Iris.

Kick threw both hands in the air and cheered. 'Cool!'

Somehow they got lost after the service station and ended up getting to Camp Melody almost an hour after the official sign-in time.

Iris stood by the car and looked over to the cabins. There were kids running everywhere, and a pillow fight had broken out on the lawn.

Iris's dad was unpacking her things from the boot when a young woman with very short hair and a clipboard walked over.

'Hello,' she said. 'You must be Iris? You're the last one to tick off my list! I'm Amber, your cabin leader.'

Iris suddenly felt shy and couldn't think of a thing to say. She wasn't sure what a cabin leader was, and that started her thinking about all the other things she didn't know. Like, where would she sleep? Would the other kids want to be friends with her? Most importantly, would they be better musicians than she was?

Iris felt goose pimples prickle over her skin.

What will
the other kids
be like?

Amber didn't seem to notice. 'Because
you're a bit late,' Amber continued, 'all the
rooms have been allocated. Don't worry,
though. You're in with a really great group

of girls. They were all here last year, so they can help you find your way around.'

Amber picked up Iris's saxophone case. 'Come on, I'll show you where you are sleeping.'

Iris turned around to pick up her backpack. Kick and her mum had wandered over to look at the river, but her dad was still with her. He had her pillow and sleeping bag.

'Let's go, kiddo,' he smiled.

Iris smiled back, but it felt a bit wonky on her face. She really, truly, absolutely wanted to be at music camp. But she also wanted to jump straight back in the car and yell, 'Step on it, Dad!'

Because no matter how much she wanted to be there, four days was a long time if she didn't fit in.

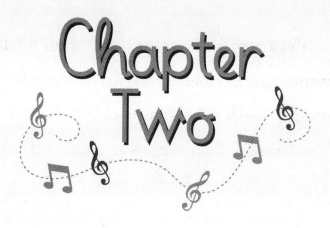

Chapter Two

Iris followed Amber across the grass to the cabins. Mobs of kids were running around, laughing, throwing balls and telling jokes. *They're probably all best friends from last year,* thought Iris. *I'm probably the only new one.*

The cabins were solid little wooden houses, each painted a different colour. Iris squared her shoulders and walked a bit faster to catch up with Amber. As she walked, she talked sternly to herself. *So what if you're the only new one? You'll only be new for today. By tomorrow, everyone will be the same. All you have to do is smile ...*

She was still encouraging herself when Amber swung open the door to the red cabin. As the sunlight spilled inside, Iris saw three girls sitting on one of the top bunks. They all jumped with surprise. They looked like they had been interrupted in the middle of a secret meeting.

Iris's smile slipped a fraction. She didn't want her first meeting with her new bunk-mates to be spoiled by bad timing. Or by an embarrassing dad!

Just as she thought that, her dad pushed past her into the cabin and looked around brightly. 'Hello! This is cosy!' he boomed. 'Where shall I put your bags, chook?'

Iris grimaced. Chook! 'Just put them anywhere,' she muttered. 'I'll work it out later.'

But she needn't have worried. The three girls on the bunk were as great as Amber had promised. Instead of carrying on whispering, or giving her nasty looks for barging in, they were all smiling, waiting to meet her.

'Girls,' said Amber. 'This is Iris. Why don't you come down and help her unpack?'

Two of the girls climbed down the

ladder, but the third jumped over the side of the bunk and landed with a thud at Iris's feet.

'Hi,' she said, smiling broadly as she pushed her long fringe off her face. 'I'm Siri. I play viola.'

The other two came and stood beside Siri. One was tall, pale and shy-looking. The other girl had short dark-brown hair, and somehow Iris could tell that she was very kind.

'I'm Annabelle,' said the kind-looking one. 'I play violin. And this is Freya,' she said, pointing to the shy girl.

'Hi,' Freya said quietly. 'I play cello.'

Iris almost laughed with relief. It was

just like school! Siri was the loud, cheeky one, Freya was the shy and gentle one, and Annabelle was much like her best friend Zoe.

'I play sax,' said Iris, grinning.

'Oh, oh! Can I have a go, *please?*' begged Siri. 'I've always wanted to play sax!'

Iris did laugh then. She was going to fit in perfectly.

Chapter Three

'Well, Iris,' said her dad. 'It's time Mum and Kick and I got going. Will you come and say goodbye?'

Iris had almost forgotten her dad was standing there. She had been too busy checking out her bunk and letting Annabelle show her which shelves in the cupboard were hers.

'I'll come with you,' said Annabelle.

'Then I can show you the music rooms on the way back.'

Iris was pleased. It wouldn't feel like such a big deal watching her family drive off if she had someone with her.

Her mum and Kick were waiting by the car. Kick was practising his handstands, but kept tumbling over onto the grass.

Annabelle stood aside to let Iris hug her mum and dad. Annabelle pretended not to notice when Iris wiped away a tear while hugging her mum.

And then the car was pulling away and Kick was waving out the open window. Iris wouldn't see them again until the night of the concert.

'Come on,' said Annabelle, when the car had disappeared. 'I'll show you around.'

They walked together across the lawn towards the hall and the music rooms. A bell rang in the distance, and Iris saw kids running out of the cabins and towards the hall.

'Morning meeting!' said Annabelle. 'Let's go!'

Iris ran after her, leaping over the grass and feeling light and free.

Chapter Four

At morning meeting, Iris had her first chance to meet all the camp leaders and kids. It was a massive group and, as she sat down in the circle of chairs, Iris began to feel shy again. She looked across the room and saw Amber give her a wink.

A grey-haired lady stood up. 'Hello, and welcome to Camp Melody,' she said. 'My name, for all you newbies, is Libby. For all you old hands, welcome back! It's good to see you again. As usual, we are going to start off with a run-through of the camp rules and our schedule. Then we'll have morning tea. This is a chance for you to start working out who you would like to perform with at the concert.'

Iris felt jumping beans of excitement in her stomach.

'Remember,' Libby went on, 'your cabin leaders are also here as music tutors, so if you have any trouble finding a group, make sure you ask for help. Now, here are our leaders!'

Around the circle, each cabin leader stood up and said their name and which instruments they tutored. When it was Amber's turn, she said she'd have a go at almost anything except bagpipes. Everyone laughed, and Iris wondered what instrument Amber really played.

Then Libby posted up the camp program.

7.30   breakfast
8.30   music tutorial
10.30 morning tea
11.00 orchestra
1.00   lunch
2.00   activities (bushwalking, rock-climbing, canoeing, football, tennis, painting)
4.00   afternoon tea and free time until dinner
7.00   dinner

'Obviously, today is a bit different,' said Libby. 'To find the right people to perform with for the concert, you have to get to know each other. So, everybody up! Push your chairs back against the wall.'

There was a terrible screeching of chair legs on the wooden floor as the space was cleared.

'OK, everybody at this end of the hall – run! Now, run to the other end of the hall, but – *wait for it!* – only if you play *flute!*'

All the flute kids raced, pounding to the far end of the hall while the rest of the camp cheered.

'That's my group!' yelled Adam, the

woodwind tutor. 'Go, flutes! Go, flutes!'

'All right, let's see,' said Libby. 'Get ready to run and join them if you play *violin!*'

And so it went on, kids running and screaming from one end to the other, backwards and forwards. Kids who'd been playing for two years or less, then kids who played more than one instrument, then kids who'd been given their instrument by their brother or sister, then kids who were at camp for the first time ...

Iris ran and ran, the group splitting and re-splitting in a hundred different ways until everyone was puffing and mixed together.

'OK!' said Libby at last. 'Well done! It's time for morning tea. I want you all to talk to someone new and start working out who you are going to play with at the concert.'

Next to Iris, Annabelle danced with excitement. 'Come on, Iris!' she said.

'Let's find Siri and Freya. Siri's got a plan for the concert already.'

Iris figured that would be OK. After all, it was her first time at camp, so everyone was new to her, really. It wouldn't matter if she didn't make another new friend straight away, would it?

Iris and Annabelle found Siri and Freya under the fig tree by their cabin. Freya was sitting on one of the swings, while Siri swung so high on hers the chain went slack at the top of each swoop. When she saw Iris and Annabelle, she leapt out of her seat and sailed through the air, landing on the grass in front of them.

'There you are,' she said. 'Guess what?'

'What?' asked Annabelle.

'Tell them, Freya.'

Freya got up off her swing. 'I met another new girl at morning tea. Her name's Mia. She plays first violin *and* she sings *and* she said she'd like to play with us.'

'That's great!' said Annabelle.

Iris stood awkwardly while the other three talked. What about her? Did they have room for her to play, too?

Chapter Five

Iris wasn't sure what to say. Would it be rude to ask straight out if she could join in with the concert piece Siri had organised?

'Um, so what are you guys playing, anyway?' she asked.

Siri grinned and lowered her voice, checking over her shoulders as though someone might be hiding nearby, waiting to steal her idea.

'We're doing this folk song I learnt at school,' she said. 'It's great, because it's all for strings and voices, and that's exactly what we've got.'

Iris realised she was right. Siri played viola, Freya played cello, and Annabelle played second violin. And now they had Mia and her first violin. Perfect.

A perfect string quartet with no room for a big, noisy, brassy saxophone.

Annabelle saw her face and quickly said to Siri, 'What about Iris? Can we fit her in somehow?'

Siri glanced at Freya, and Freya bit her lip. They both looked uncomfortable. There was a long and horrible silence.

'Er, well …' Siri was trying to talk, but she didn't seem to know what to say. 'The thing is, Iris,' she blurted out at last, 'we didn't know you when we started planning this. We really, really like you, but I don't think a sax will work.'

'But we're singing, too,' said Freya. 'Do you want to do the singing bit with us?'

'Yeah!' said Annabelle, turning to Iris. 'Can you sing?'

Iris pulled a face. 'Not really. Not properly. Only in the shower.'

'Oh, too bad,' said Annabelle sadly.

'Yeah, too bad,' Iris agreed.

She would have to find someone else to perform with. How would she do that?

After morning tea, it was time to meet up with the tutors. Some of the kids, like Siri, Freya and Annabelle, had already decided what they were going to work on for the concert. It was easy for them. They went off to find their tutors and pick out practice rooms.

Iris looked around for any other kids like her, who didn't know where to go or who to be with. She couldn't see any.

Why did I have to play the stupid sax? she grumbled to herself. *If only I played the flute or clarinet. Something normal …*

She sat down on the grass next to her saxophone case. Inside, her sax was polished and shining, but what difference did it make how nicely it was tuned if she had no-one to play with?

She'd been so worried about getting stuck in a cabin with girls who didn't want to be friends, she hadn't thought to worry about the concert. Boy, had she got it backwards!

Chapter Six

Sitting on the ground, picking seed heads off the grass and flicking them at her sax, Iris sulked.

She wasn't usually a sulker, but today she thought she deserved some time-out to feel sorry for herself. She'd come to camp all by herself. She'd been brave and friendly and done her best to make friends. So why had she still ended up with no-one to play with?

'Iris?' said Amber, walking over from one of the practice rooms. 'What are you doing out here by yourself?'

Iris shrugged. She didn't want to make a big deal out of it, but she was sure Amber would feel bad for her when she knew that Iris had been left out.

'Why didn't you come and find me?' asked Amber. 'If you were having trouble you should have come to me at once. Now you've missed out on heaps of your first tutorial! Up you get.'

'But there's no-one for me to play with,' Iris protested. She was surprised that Amber didn't seem to understand that this wasn't her fault. She picked up her sax.

'No-one in your cabin, you mean. Or no-one you've met yet. There are heaps of other kids to play with, though.'

'Aren't they all already in groups?'

Amber gave her a lopsided smile. 'Luckily for you, no. In fact, I was on my way to find you because I have two kids still left over and trying to work out what they're going to do. I think you might be able to help each other out.'

Help out the left-overs? thought Iris. *I want to be in a proper group, not just stuck with a bunch of left-overs.*

But it was too late. Iris had wasted morning tea feeling disappointed and sulky, and now she was a left-over, too.

'After you,' said Amber, standing to one side of the practice room door so Iris could go in first.

Iris took a deep breath. Sitting inside,

looking glum, were two kids. Iris was surprised to see that they were both older. One was a girl with long hair, and the other was a boy with a pimple on the very end of his nose. They sat up straighter when they saw Amber.

'Here she is,' said Amber. 'This is Iris, here with her sax. Iris, this is Jess, who plays drum. And Caleb, who plays guitar.'

'Hi, Iris,' said Jess. She still looked unhappy, but at least she was trying to be nice. Unlike Caleb, who just scowled.

Iris swallowed hard. This didn't look good at all ...

'OK,' said Amber. 'I'll leave you to it for now. You guys talk about ideas for the concert. Tomorrow is our first proper tutorial where we'll start preparing the piece you've chosen. For now, have some fun getting to know each other and finding out what sort of music you'd like to play.'

They all nodded obediently, and then Amber was gone.

Have fun? thought Iris. *Not likely.*

She ought to make an effort, though. She was about to sit down next to Jess when Caleb started complaining.

'A sax?' he said. 'How's that going to work?' Without waiting for a reply, he went on. 'It's not going to work at all. Forget what Amber said. We might as well skip the concert altogether. No-one will notice if we don't play, and we can just spend the rest of the week practising by ourselves.'

'What?' gasped Iris.

It was bad enough being stuck with left-overs, but even the left-overs didn't want her! How dare they? There was no way she'd come to Camp Melody to miss out on the concert!

Chapter Seven

Before Iris could tell Caleb just exactly what she thought of his suggestion, Jess spoke up.

'Shut up, Caleb. Just because you're in a bad mood, there's no reason to take it out on Iris.'

'What?' Caleb looked surprised. 'I wasn't taking anything out on anyone! Sorry, Iris. Sax is cool and all, but let's face it, what can the three of us play together?'

Iris and Jess looked at each other.

'I mean, look at us,' Caleb continued. 'Iris, your sax is for jazz, and Jess, you've got an African drum. As for me, I've got a twelve-stringed classical guitar. I don't see what sort of music we could put together out of that.'

Iris struggled. She felt like throwing up her hands and saying, *I know! It's hopeless!* At the same time, though, she wanted to snap back at Caleb, *Don't be such a quitter! Of course we can do something.*

Except she couldn't think what, so it wasn't a very convincing thing to say.

Jess seemed to be having similar

thoughts. 'You might be right, Caleb, but shouldn't we at least try?'

Caleb sighed. 'Go on, then. We'll try. It won't be any good, of course, but we might as well do something to fill in the time …'

Iris rolled her eyes.

What a moaner!

Jess saw her and smiled. She rolled her eyes, too, and then the two of them almost got the giggles.

'Ahem!' said Iris, bending over to fiddle with her sax case so Caleb wouldn't see she was biting her lip to stop laughing.

Jess concentrated seriously on nothing at all out the music room window.

'Well, come on, you two,' said Caleb, in what Iris's mum would have called a *wounded soldier* voice. 'It's pointless, but let's make a start.'

It was too much. Iris and Jess burst out laughing, and once they started they couldn't stop. Jess was holding her stomach in agony, and Iris had tears in her eyes.

Caleb looked at them blankly. 'Oh, terrific,' he said, with a weary sigh. 'Now on top of everything else, it turns out you're both completely mental.'

At lunchtime, Iris met up again with Annabelle, Siri and Freya as they stood in line for hamburgers.

'We talked about every single piece of music we'd ever heard, and we still couldn't find anything we could play together!' she told them. 'And I mean really *nothing*. I don't know what we'll tell Amber tomorrow.'

'Oh, that's such hard luck,' said Annabelle kindly.

'Yeah, well ...' said Iris. 'Anyway, how did you guys go?'

'Great!' said Siri. 'We've got Mel as our tutor, and she's tops, and Mia fits in perfectly.'

'Really?'

'Yeah, it's so funny because we all play at the same grade and she's even got the same type of violin as Annabelle. Plus her voice harmonises excellently with ours.'

'Oh, good,' said Iris, feeling a bit jealous.

'Are Jess and Caleb nice?' asked Annabelle.

Iris looked over to where Jess was eating

with some of the older girls. She spotted
Caleb slouching at the back of the queue,
obviously complaining about something
to his friend, who was laughing.

'Yeah,' she sighed. 'They're nice.'

So far, everyone on camp had been nice,
one way or the other (Caleb was the other!),
but being nice wasn't going to be enough
when they got on stage in three days.

Chapter Eight

After lunch, half the kids went bushwalking while the others went rock-climbing. Iris was in the bushwalking group, along with the rest of her cabin and Mia. They were fast becoming a gang.

'All right, you lot,' said Libby, who was leading the walk. 'Stay on the path and try not to fall too far behind. We're headed for the top of that hill over there.'

For a while, Iris was able to forget about the concert. She fell into step with the other girls and soon they were all puffing and laughing, tripping over the uneven track and telling music jokes.

'Hey, Annabelle,' said Mia. 'How do you keep your violin from getting stolen?'

'I don't know,' Annabelle smiled.

'Put it in a viola case.'

'Oh, ha, ha, very funny, I'm sure,' said Siri. 'Well, tell me, Mia, which is smaller – a violin or a viola?'

'A violin, of course,' said Mia.

'Ah, no. They're actually the same size, only the violinist's head is so much bigger.'

'Oooh!'

Iris laughed. The jokes were terrible, but bad jokes had always made her laugh, and Mia and Siri knew hundreds.

At the top of the hill, they stood and looked over the valley. Iris could see the red cabin she was staying in. It looked like a matchbox.

'We came a long way,' she said to Annabelle.

'I know, but we'll have to get back quickly now or we'll miss out on the good biscuits at afternoon tea.'

'Afternoon tea?' yelled Siri, overhearing them. 'Let's go, guys!'

Shrieking and whooping, they pelted back down the hill to the dinner hall.

Free time that afternoon was glorious. Iris felt like she'd been on camp with her new friends forever. Some of the kids were playing French cricket with a garbage can as the wicket, but Iris sneaked off with Annabelle and the others to a secret spot by the river that the girls had discovered the year before.

Just past the dinner hall, close enough to hear the dinner bell but far enough away to be quite on their own, they sat along the riverbank and told stories. They sat there and talked until the sun started to go down.

'It's getting chilly now,' said Iris.

'Yeah, and I've had six mozzie bites in the last five minutes,' said Annabelle.

'Me too,' said Freya. 'Let's go back before anyone looks for us and finds our secret spot.'

As they got up and brushed twigs and leaves off their numb bottoms, they heard the dinner bell ring. Siri yelped. Iris thought Siri must either be constantly hungry, or else she didn't believe there would be enough food for all of them.

'Run, guys! It's dinner time!'

They arrived at the hall in time to bags a table near the door. They all sat down, feeling pleased with themselves. And then Jess and Caleb walked in, looking around for Iris. Her heart sank. Just when she'd forgotten about the concert!

Jess spotted her and walked over.

'So, Iris, what are we going to tell Amber tomorrow?'

'Urgh, I don't know. It's like we haven't done our homework, isn't it?'

'Yeah, I know,' said Caleb. 'And we'll probably get into a lot of trouble.'

Iris and Jess rolled their eyes at each other.

'This must have happened before though, right?' asked Siri. 'They must have emergency back-up music or something, surely.'

'I hope so,' said Iris. 'I mean, I'm sure they do.'

Caleb sighed sorrowfully. 'We'll soon find out, one way or the other.'

Chapter Nine

Iris was so worried about her tutorial with Amber, she didn't sleep well. She kept having awful dreams about the concert. She dreamt she'd forgotten the music, or she'd forgotten how to play her sax. In the worst dream of all, she was on stage in her undies, trying to sing opera!

By morning, she was exhausted. She

felt like she hadn't slept at all. She hopped out of bed and got dressed while the other three slept.

Maybe if I go for a walk I'll suddenly get a brilliant idea for the concert, she thought.

Nope.

She walked around the camp until her sneakers were soaked through with dew, but she had no useful thoughts. She didn't have a watch on but it felt late so she headed back to the dinner hall.

At breakfast, she waved hello to Annabelle and the gang and then went over to Jess and Caleb. They were sitting together, and Jess was poking at her soggy cornflakes with a spoon.

'What are we going to do?' Jess wailed when she saw Iris. 'All I can think about is the fact that we have to tell Amber we don't have anything to play.'

'Me, too,' said Iris. 'I've been wracking my brains.'

Caleb was wolfing down scrambled eggs and toast. For the first time since Iris had met him, he seemed almost cheerful.

Typical, thought Iris. *He's probably happiest when things go wrong.*

At the front of the hall, Libby stood up and clapped her hands.

'Breakfast will be over in ten minutes. That gives you five to finish eating and five to clear the tables and bring your plates and bowls over to the kitchen. You then have two and a half minutes to brush your teeth and grab your instruments before tutorials. Your time starts — *now!*'

Iris, Jess and Caleb looked at each other. Twelve and a half minutes until they had to face Amber.

'So,' said Amber. 'What have you guys got to show me?'

Iris scrunched her eyes shut. Hopefully she'd wake up any second now ...

'Nothing,' said Caleb bluntly. 'We've got nothing.'

'Girls?'

Iris and Jess shrugged.

'It's true,' said Jess. 'We talked and talked and really tried, but we can't think of anything we can play together.'

Iris waited for Amber to say something. To say she understood, perhaps. But Amber just folded her arms and waited.

'We really did try,' said Iris. 'But it's not easy, you know. We've all got tricky instruments ...'

Amber raised an eyebrow. She didn't look like she felt sorry for them. She looked disappointed. 'Of course it's not easy,' she said. 'I never thought it would be. I did think, though, that kids imaginative enough to play unusual instruments would be able to come up with at least *one tune* to play for the concert.'

'We did our best,' Caleb protested.

'Did you? You really, truly tried your best, and you really think there's *nothing* you can play?'

Iris bit her lip. She *thought* that was right, but it sounded silly when Amber said it like that.

Amber went on. 'You couldn't even play *Twinkle, Twinkle, Little Star*?'

Caleb laughed. 'I guess we could do *that*, but we want to play something good, not some dumb baby tune.'

Amber breathed out through her nose. It wasn't exactly a snort, but it was very close. 'So what you really mean is there *is* music you could play together, but you'd rather sit around like lumps and not play anything unless you think the other kids will be impressed. Is that it?'

Iris blinked. Was Amber right?

'Well, yeah!' said Caleb. 'Of course we want to play something cool. Of course we don't want to look like losers in front of everyone!'

Amber gaped at him. 'Losers! What are you talking about? We're here to make music – what's that got to do with winning or losing? It's not a competition!

'And as you've brought up looking cool, Caleb, I have to say there's nothing cool about feeling sorry for yourselves.'

Iris gulped. Amber was right!

Amber sighed. 'Look, I know you

probably think I don't know what I'm talking about, but I do understand. When I was your age, everyone played flute. But what do you think I played?'

Aha! Now Iris would find out!

'Not the bagpipes, right?'

'Definitely not the bagpipes, but you are pretty close.'

'Trombone?'

'Banjo?'

'Ha! I wish!' laughed Amber. 'No, I had an accordion.'

'Ooh!' They all flinched in sympathy.

'Yeah,' Amber went on. 'And you know what they say — what's the difference between an accordion and an onion?'

'What?'

'Nobody cries when you chop up an accordion.'

Iris laughed.

'Now,' said Amber. 'Let's get to work. We've got a concert to play in three days and no time to waste!'

Chapter Ten

It was amazing, Iris thought, how quickly things could turn around. At breakfast, she'd been feeling awful. Now it was morning tea, and she had never felt better. She hummed to herself in the queue for muffins and cordial.

'What are you humming?' asked a voice behind her.

'Oh, Annabelle! We just had the best tutorial! I'm so relieved!'

'So what are you going to play? You did end up with something, right?'

'Mmm,' Iris smiled. 'We're all set.'

'Go on — tell. Is it something I'd know?'

Iris laughed. 'Oh, yeah, you'd know it, but I'm not telling. You'll just have to wait and see.'

'I bet it's something cool, though?'

Iris smiled mysteriously. *Cool* wasn't quite the right word. In fact, it was quite likely that their performance was going to be the exact opposite of cool, but she wasn't worried about that anymore. Like Amber said, being cool wasn't everything.

The point was, she was going to make music. She was going to take something as ordinary as her breath and turn it into a sound that made other people want to dance or clap or cry or dream …

And that wasn't cool. That, if you thought about it, was amazing.

That afternoon, it was Iris and the gang's turn to go rock-climbing.

'No way!' shrieked Siri. 'What if I split a nail or get a blister? That would be a disaster for my playing!'

Mia jabbed her in the ribs with her elbow. 'Oh, don't worry, Siri. You know, if worst comes to worst, I know how to make my violin sound like a viola.'

'Really? And how's that?'

'I'll just sit at the back and not play.'

'Hey!' squeaked Siri. 'You think that's funny do you?' She chased Mia across the lawn.

It was another bright clear day. Iris smiled to herself and thought of Kick and her mum and dad.

I expected to miss them more, Iris thought. *I thought I'd have a good time, but I also thought I'd be homesick. I never guessed I'd like camp as much as this.*

'Oi! Iris!' yelled Siri. 'Are you coming or not?'

Iris blinked herself back into the world. The others were ahead of her, looking back and waiting.

Annabelle smiled warmly. 'She's just

daydreaming, Siri,' she said. 'You don't have to be so bossy.'

'Me? *Bossy?*' Siri pretended to be shocked. 'Iris, back me up. I'm not bossy, am I?'

'No, of course not,' laughed Iris, catching up. 'You're a shy little rose petal.'

'See?' Siri said to Annabelle, linking her arm through Iris's. 'Now, pull yourselves together, girls – it's time for a chorus line.'

One after the other, Annabelle, Freya and Mia linked their arms until all five girls were standing shoulder to shoulder.

'On the count of three,' said Siri. 'A-one, a-two, a-one two three – '

Everywhere we go-oh
People want to know-oh
Who we are-ah
And where we come from
And if they don't hear us
We shout a little louder!

And they high-kicked the rest of the way to the rock-climbing wall, yelling at the top of their voices. The song echoed across the valley.

Chapter Eleven

The rest of Camp Melody went by far too quickly. Time somehow sped up and plonked Iris down on the last day of camp.

In between the other music classes, everyone had been practising madly for the concert. Each day, fewer people lazed around on the grass at free time, and more of them went back to the practice rooms.

Iris, Jess and Caleb practised after dinner, too.

At their final rehearsal, Amber was encouraging them to relax with their music and have fun. 'Don't be so stressy,' she reminded them. 'It's not a contest. I'd rather you guys had a good time than get every single note absolutely perfect. I'd rather you played with some heart.'

Iris knew what Amber meant, but it was hard not to stress when you were performing in front of so many people. As Caleb had said, of *course* they wanted it to sound good!

But as they practised for the last time, Iris suddenly got it. If she got every single

note right, then the music would be perfect. But what if she made every note sing out with feeling?

If she could play like that, it would be better than perfect. It would be *magical*.

She felt her fingers move over the keys more lightly and easily than ever, and without noticing it, she began to sway with her playing. She imagined her sax was singing about sitting by the river with Annabelle and the gang, and watching Siri fly off the swing, and listening to Mia's jokes …

Before Iris knew it, Amber was on her feet and clapping wildly.

'You guys are awesome!' she cheered.

'Wow! I can't believe you're the same three kids who thought you couldn't make music together!'

Iris looked at Jess and Caleb. They smiled at each other shyly.

'Thanks, Amber,' said Iris. 'We couldn't have done it without you.'

'Are you crazy? I wouldn't have missed this for anything. And Iris, I have to say, that was above and beyond anything I've heard you play so far.'

Iris grinned. She couldn't wait to get on stage.

Gulp. Now that the time had come, Iris was feeling pretty nervous. She *always* felt nervous before a concert. She *knew* she always felt nervous, but somehow that never made it any better.

The little red cabin was a mess. Annabelle, Siri, Freya and Mia were all giggling with their own nerves as they got their costumes ready. Annabelle had brought four identical white shirts for them to wear, and Freya was tying lengths of gold ribbon around each girl's waist like a belt.

Iris looked up from where she was doing her hair in the mirror. 'You guys look great!' she said. 'Like a proper quartet, all matching.'

Annabelle smiled back. 'Your hair looks cool.'

Iris had braided her hair into tiny plaits, and was threading coloured beads onto the ends. When she moved her head, she could hear the beads clinking together gently. She had put on her concert outfit already — a pink shirt and her favourite jeans.

'Iris!' called a voice. It was Jess, standing by the cabin door. 'Are you ready?'

Iris looked over and saw that Jess was wearing a long blue dress and a chunky beaded necklace. Behind her, Caleb was wearing all black — black jeans, black T-shirt and old black sneakers.

She laughed. They looked just like their music! Nobody matched — they were all wearing different things in different colours, and yet somehow they sort of went together, too.

'I'm ready! Just let me grab my sax.'

There was no time for nerves now!

Chapter Twelve

On the way to the hall, Iris caught a glimpse of her parents and Kick getting out of their car, but then Jess and Caleb whisked her away backstage.

The dining hall had been cleared and filled with rows of chairs. A curtain was strung up at one end to hide all the performers between acts. Libby was making sure all the stage lights were working, and

Amber and some of the other tutors were handing out programs at the door.

Behind the curtain, the older kids kept hissing, 'Shh! Shh! The audience will hear you if you're too noisy!'

But they didn't have a hope. Half the kids were busy tuning up, and the other half were trying to talk loudly enough and fast enough to chase away their nerves.

Iris clenched her teeth and jiggled her legs. Jess and Caleb were going through the program to double-check where they were. As if they could forget – lucky last!

Annabelle, Siri, Freya and Mia were on first. They were standing closest to the curtain, ready to go on as soon as Libby gave them the signal. Iris wasn't sure what the signal was, but the hall suddenly went quiet.

The concert had begun!

Annabelle and the gang waited for their names to be announced and then walked out on stage. Iris saw them disappear through the curtain, and held her breath.

There was a long pause, and then Siri began to sing. A soft, skipping sort of tune. The others joined in, one by one, until all four of them were singing in a round. Then one by one, the instruments joined in, too.

Iris had never heard anything so beautiful. It was kind of sad and hopeful at the same time, with no beginning or end. Just one lovely circle of sound. Iris couldn't believe she'd been sleeping in the same room as these amazing girls!

When they finished, Iris clapped so hard her hands stung.

'Careful,' said Caleb. 'Don't want you to bruise your fingers until we've done our bit.'

Iris and Jess rolled their eyes at him and went on clapping.

Iris was standing backstage listening to a trumpet solo when Jess tugged on her sleeve. 'That was the second to last performance. We're next!'

They looked at each other and started jumping up and down, flapping their arms and wobbling their heads.

'What are you crazy girls up to now?' asked Caleb.

'Shaking out the nerves, of course,' Iris whispered back at him.

'Well, you can stop it right now. They're clapping, which means we'll be on stage in ten seconds.'

Iris and Jess stopped jumping and picked up their instruments.

'Our last act is a three-piece band, featuring saxophone, African drum and classical guitar,' they heard Libby announce. 'May I introduce … The Left-overs!'

Here goes, thought Iris.

The moment Iris stepped out from behind the curtain and into the light, her nerves vanished. She could hear the audience shuffling in their seats, but the bright stage lights meant she could only see Jess and Caleb. There were two chairs — one for Jess and one for Caleb. She would stand.

'Ready?' whispered Jess, setting her drum between her knees. She began tapping out a lolloping beat, like a rabbit hip-hopping across the lawn.

Iris tapped her foot along with it, and then Caleb started plucking out the melody on his guitar. There was a little pause, and then some laughter as the audience recognised the tune.

It was *Twinkle, Twinkle, Little Star*. But it was nothing like what anyone had heard before.

Jess hit her drum faster, and Caleb's delicate picking became a rock and roll strum, and then Iris closed her eyes and let her saxophone sing out over the top. The sax swooped and soared, and as it sang, Iris heard herself telling the audience about how three left-over kids had learned to fit together in a totally new way.

As they played, Iris wished it could last forever, but all too soon, it was over.

After the concert, there was a supper
before everyone went home.

Iris's mum and dad pushed their way
through the crowd, beaming and waving.
'Darling! You were incredible! I never
knew you could play like that!' Iris's mum
had tears in her eyes.

'I didn't either,' grinned Iris.

'Well done,' said her dad, giving her a
crushing hug. 'I'm so proud of you.'

'Where's Kick?' Iris asked, looking
around.

'Oh, he ran off to find your friend and
try her drum.'

'Iris!'

Iris turned to see who had called her, and saw Amber edging sideways between groups of people. She had both hands high over her head, holding plates above the crowd.

'I brought you some cake,' she said, before she noticed Iris's parents. 'Hey, wasn't Iris something?'

'She sure was!'

'What sort of thing?' teased Iris.

'Well, what would the word be?' her dad teased back.

'Look, here's Kick. Let's ask him. Hey, Kick – what did you think of your sister with her sax?'

Kick gave one of his hugest smiles and two thumbs up.

'*Cool!*' he yelled. 'Iris is totally cool!'

Iris laughed and laughed.

So much for worrying they'd look silly at the concert! Maybe music wasn't about winning or losing, or even being cool or not cool, but right now, Iris felt on top of the world!

Flower Girl

by
Chrissie Perry

Illustrations by
Aki Fukuoka

Chapter One

'Hold still, Lola! If you keep wriggling around like that, Katya won't be able to get your proper measurements.'

Lola giggled. 'But it *tickles,* Mum,' she said. Her mum grinned back as Katya wrapped the tape measure around Lola's waist. Lola's eyes scanned the room.

A big rack in the corner held lots of long dresses. Lola thought they all looked beautiful. She could see a dress with a frill that flicked out, almost touching the ground. If she crouched down from the stool she was standing on, she could see the sequins on the neckline of a powder-blue dress on the end of the rack. They glittered like a thousand tiny stars, as though someone had pulled them out of the sky and sewn them on ...

'Lola, can you stand straight and tall for Katya?' Lola's mum asked.

'If I measure you while you're bobbing down like that, we'll end up with a mini-dress,' said Katya.

'Oops, sorry,' Lola said, straightening up so that Katya could measure the length from her waist to her knees.

'So, let's see,' Katya said with a smile, glancing down at the picture that Lola and her mum had drawn together. 'I think I may have the perfect fabric for this dress. Wait here for a minute.'

As Katya ducked into the back room, Lola jumped down from the little stool and bumped, *smack*, into something.

The *something* she'd bumped into was a dressmaker's dummy.

'Oh, hello Headless,' she joked.

There were three dressmaker's dummies scattered around the room. They had no heads, and where their legs should have been was a pole on a stand.

Two of the dummies wore half-finished

dresses, but the one Lola bumped into was completely undressed, except for a thousand pins with pearl tips sticking into her.

'Ouch, you poor thing,' Lola laughed, nodding at Headless. 'But don't you think you should put some clothes on?'

'Headless is going to help me with a wedding gown this afternoon,' explained Katya. She stood at the door with her hands behind her back. 'So, ladies,' said Katya. 'Are you ready to see what I found? It's pretty special.'

Lola clasped both hands together when she saw what Katya was holding.

'Oh, it's … it's …' Lola searched for the right word. Beautiful? Lovely? No word seemed quite good enough to describe the fabric Katya was holding out.

It was Lola's favourite colour in the whole world. Purple! The exact type of purple Lola had dreamt her dress would be. Not a mushy mauve, but something deeper and stronger … like a violet. As Katya pulled the material from the giant roll, Lola reached out to touch it. It was soft and smooth.

'So, do you think this is OK?' Katya asked.

Lola sighed dreamily. 'It's *perfect*,' she said.

'Good,' Katya replied, picking up the drawing Lola and her mum had drawn.

'When you come back in two weeks, I'll have your dress ready for a fitting. Then, you can pick it up the week after that.'

Lola screwed up her nose. Three weeks seemed a very long time to wait for her dress. She'd imagined herself walking out of the dressmaker's with a beautiful gown, just like the one they had drawn.

It seemed a little bit magic that you could draw a dress on a piece of paper, and someone could make it real for you. Almost like having a fairy godmother. Even if *this* fairy godmother was a little bit slow!

'That might feel like a long time,' Katya said, as though reading Lola's mind, 'but to make a special dress like this, I have to first create a pattern, then cut it out, then sew it all together.'

As she spoke, Katya pointed past Headless to a large work table with scissors and brown cardboard and a sewing machine. That type of magic looked like a lot of hard work.

'But I promise you, Lola,' Katya said kindly, 'the next time you come in you'll be able to get an idea of how pretty you're going to look. Now, I'm just going to pop out the back again to get my notebook.'

As Katya left the room, Lola lifted the fabric and watched how it sort of floated down to the work table.

'I can't believe it's actually going to happen, Mum,' she squealed.

'Me neither,' her mum laughed back, giving Lola a huge squeeze. 'It's like a dream come true!'

Chapter Two

As Lola hugged her mum, she thought back to the moment she'd first found out.

Lola and Will had just come back from their karate class. She had been *starving* and the smell of a roast dinner in the oven was almost too much to bear. Lola's mum, Helen, was humming a tune in the kitchen while Rex chopped up some beans.

As soon as her mum walked into the lounge room, Lola knew something was up. Her mum was smiling, and the way she kept looking at Rex was different, somehow.

'Guys. Sit down. We've got some news,' she said.

Lola sneaked a look at Will. He was doing his eyebrow thing. Will always raised his eyebrows when he was wondering about something. When he and Rex had first moved in, it used to annoy Lola. Now she was used to it and even kind of liked it.

Lola sat next to Will and his raised eyebrows.

'Well,' Rex began in a very serious voice, 'you know that Helen and I love each other very much.'

'Daaad,' Will groaned.

Rex chuckled. 'Sorry, mate,' he said, ruffling Will's hair. 'The thing is ...'

He smiled at Lola's mum and his voice trailed off.

'The thing is,' Lola's mum picked up, 'we've decided, well, as long as you kids are OK with it ...'

Lola threw her hands up in the air. 'What have you decided?' she asked. Really, for grown-ups, the two of them were acting kind of silly.

'We've decided ...' Rex said.

'To get married!' Lola's mum exclaimed.

'OK, Helen,' Katya said, sitting at the work table with her notebook ready. 'Did you get the measurements of the other flower girl? The one who lives interstate?'

'Yes,' Lola's mum said, fishing around in her handbag for a piece of paper. 'These are Tess's measurements.'

Lola scratched her head as Katya jotted the figures into her notebook. She had been so excited when her mum asked her to be a flower girl that she'd almost forgotten to breathe. She'd only ever been to one wedding before. It had been pretty cool. But *this* wedding was going to be the absolute coolest day of her entire life!

In fact, she'd been so excited about it that she'd almost forgotten there was going to be a *second* flower girl.

Tess was Will's cousin, and she was going to fly down with her family the week before the big wedding.

It was kind of weird to think that Will had cousins Lola hadn't even met. All Lola knew was that Tess was a few years younger than her, and that she had a brother who was going to be a paige boy with Will.

Lola grinned to herself. She knew lots of girls from school who were about Tess's age. Her favourite was a little girl who was blonde and cute and a bit shy. Sometimes, Lola and her friends let her join in their games at lunchtime.

Maybe Tess would be just like that?

'Thanks, Katya,' Lola's mum interrupted her thoughts. 'Hot chocolate time, Lola?'

Lola nodded, and thoughts about Tess flew out of her mind.

For the moment, anyway.

Chapter Three

Later that afternoon, Lola sat with her mum and her best friend Abbey in the lounge room. About a thousand magazines were strewn all over the coffee table. Will concentrated on tapping the buttons of his Game Boy. The tapping sound ran around the room.

Abbey pushed her hair back and let out a massive sigh.

'You are the luckiest duck in the universe, Loles!' she said. 'I wish *my* mum and dad would get married.'

'But they're already married,' Lola's mum reminded her.

'Then I wish they'd get married *again*,' Abbey giggled.

Lola's mum laughed. 'Well,' she said, 'the wedding will be fun. But there's a lot to organise. I definitely need a cup of tea before I continue.'

'Yes please,' Lola and Abbey said together.

'Waiter, can I have a glass of milk?' Will added cheekily, continuing his Game Boy *tap, tap, tap*.

Lola's mum rolled her eyes. 'OK Loles, while I'm gone, maybe you can have a look at some flowers for you and Tess. Perhaps you could come up with some ideas of what might go with your purple dresses.'

As soon as Lola's mum had left the room, Abbey started acting crazy. 'Look what I found,' she whispered.

Lola stared as Abbey pulled out a brochure that was tucked away in the back of a bridal magazine. She noticed the title first. 'Hawaiian Honeymoon Bliss' was written in big, bold letters across the top of the brochure. Underneath the words, there was a picture of a lovely beach with golden sands and bright blue water.

Abbey pointed to it about a hundred times. Then she flipped the brochure over to the back page.

Written in black texta in her mum's handwriting were two dates. Lola noticed that the first date was the day after the wedding.

Lola could already imagine swimming in the clear water with Will, building huge sandcastles, eating cold ice-creams ...

'Awesome!' she exclaimed loudly. 'We're going to Hawaii!'

Will paused from tapping his Game Boy and leant over to look at the brochure.

'Loles,' he said slowly, 'it's a *honeymoon*. Dad and your mum are going. Not us.

That's why Aunty Kay is coming with Beau and Tess. So she can look after us.'

I want to go on holiday!

Lola watched as her mum came back into the lounge room with the tray of drinks. She kept watching her mum as she sneaked two spoonfuls of sugar in her tea.

'So, what do you think of these flowers, Loles?' her mum asked, pointing at a picture.

Lola breathed in. The flowers were *perfect*. Some of them were light pink, and others were purple. They were tied with a green bow that looked great with the green leaves.

But, right now, she couldn't stop thinking about what Will had said.

'Mum,' she said slowly, 'is it true? Are you and Rex going on a honeymoon without us?' Lola reached for a third spoonful of sugar as she spoke. Normally her mum wouldn't let her have three whole spoonfuls in her tea. But she didn't say anything about it this time.

'Oh, sweetie,' Lola's mum said. 'I'm sorry. It's just been so crazy lately. I thought

I told you that Will's Aunty Kay was coming with Beau and Tess to look after you while Rex and I go on our honeymoon.'

Lola reached for a fourth spoonful of sugar, but this time her mum pushed the bowl away.

'Loles, Rex and I are going away together. We haven't had much time to be on our own, and it's only for a week …'

'I'll be here,' Abbey said brightly. 'And you're going to have a brand new *girl* cousin in the house. Which is pretty lucky, because I'll just be stuck with Dumb and Dumber, as usual!'

Lola felt a little smile twitching around her lips. Dumb and Dumber were Abbey's not-so-nice pet names for her brothers.

Lola drew a circle around the perfect flowers in the brochure. Then she let the twitch turn into a smile. Lola had the wedding to look forward to. And she was going to have a little girl in her house for once.

Abbey was right. She *was* the luckiest duck in the entire universe!

Chapter Four

Lola counted down the days until Will's cousins arrived. Five sleeps seemed like a very long time. But finally, she stood with her family in the Arrivals section of the airport. It was fascinating watching everyone come through the sliding doors. Some people waved and laughed as they were met by friends and family. Some cried and hugged.

'Is that them, Rex?' Lola asked for the hundredth time, jiggling her hand impatiently in his.

'No. No ... yes!' Rex said finally. 'That's them now! Just coming out of the door.'

'Beau!' Will yelled. 'Over here!'

Lola stayed close to her mum and Rex. It was a bit strange to see Aunty Kay. She looked a lot like Rex but with long hair.

Lola felt herself staring as Beau waved at Will. She'd thought that Beau would be younger than Will, since Tess was younger than her. But he actually looked about Will's age. He was wearing really baggy pants and a baseball cap that sat backwards on his head.

Then Lola looked down.

The little girl who sort of *bounced* towards them was nothing like Lola had imagined. Tess was small and thin. Her hair was jet black, and cut into a jagged bob that bounced up and down as she jogged over to them.

'Hi, Uncle Rex!' she squealed, leaping into Rex's arms so that he had to let go of Lola's hand to catch her. 'I got a colouring book on the plane! And a box of pencils! And two biscuits in little packets, but I saved one of them!'

'Did you, sweetheart?' Rex said, putting Tess on his hip while he kissed Aunty Kay and gave Beau a handshake. 'Kay, this is

Helen, and this is Lola,' he introduced. 'My girls,' he added proudly.

'It's lovely to meet you,' Aunty Kay said, giving Lola's mum a hug and then turning to Lola. 'And you too, Lola,' she said. As soon as Aunty Kay smiled, Lola liked her. Her smile was just like Rex's.

Lola watched as Tess grabbed Rex's cheeks, pulling his attention back to her.

'You know why I saved one of the biscuits, Uncle Rex?' she asked, squishing his cheeks together. Rex's smile was square between her small hands.

Lola watched as Tess jumped out of Rex's arms and landed beside her. In two seconds, there was a crumbling biscuit being pressed into her hand.

'I saved it for my new cousin!' Tess announced loudly, making sure that *everyone* was watching her. 'Lola!'

At bedtime, Lola stepped over Tess's suitcase and around the edges of the trundle bed where Tess lay. Lola's bedroom had never seemed quite so small before. Of course, she'd had people stay over. But somehow, even though Tess was tiny, she seemed to take up a lot of space.

She could hear Beau and Will talking and laughing in Will's room next door.

The boys had been playing together all day. Which had left Lola with Tess …

'Lola?' Tess said, sitting up in her bed. 'What's your favourite colour?'

Lola got into bed and yawned. She felt like she'd been asked more questions in one day than in her entire life put together.

'Ah, purple,' she said.

'Me too!' Tess said enthusiastically.

Lola snuggled under the doona and closed her eyes.

'Lola?' Tess's voice ripped into her almost-sleep. 'Which do you like better, big dogs or little dogs?'

It was hard to roll her eyes while they were closed.

I just want to go to sleep

'Little dogs,' Lola said, letting the words drift out on another yawn.

Suddenly, Lola felt her arm being yanked. She opened her eyes.

'Me too!' Tess exclaimed. 'Because you can pick them up and cuddle them.'

Lola tugged her arm back.

'Night, Tess,' she said hopefully.

'Night, Lola,' Tess replied.

Lola rolled over and let the waves of sleep wash over her. It had been a long day, and it was a gorgeous feeling to let go and drift into a deep sleep. Down, down ...

'Lola?'

Tess's voice woke her up with a jolt.

'What's your favourite animal?'

Chapter Five

'Lola, let's see whose legs are longer. Straighten yours out,' said Tess.

She and Tess were stuck in the tiny back seats of Rex's car, facing the back window.

It was time for the second dress fitting, and *everyone* was coming. Will and Beau were getting their suits from a shop a few doors down from the dressmaker's.

Rex was driving and Lola's mum sat in the front. Will and Beau sat in the middle seats with Aunty Kay. And Lola and Tess were …

'Lola!', Tess said, nudging her, '*straighten your legs out.*'

'We're here, guys,' Rex called from the driver's seat.

When he opened the door, Lola was glad to get out.

'You girls are divine!' Lola's mum exclaimed. 'Just take a look at yourselves.'

Lola stood on Katya's little stool,

with Tess on the ground in front of her. She looked down at her purple dress. Lola could feel the fabric over her shoulders. She loved the way the skirt flared at the bottom. It was really gorgeous!

She hopped off the stool and turned to look in the mirror. All she could see was her own head and a purple Tess spinning around to make herself dizzy.

'You look really pretty, Tess,' Lola said. 'Like a little princess.'

Lola's mum rubbed Lola's back in little circles. It was the sort of touch that said 'well done'. It was the sort of touch that made Lola want to lean in and give her mum a big cuddle. A cuddle that would say how much Lola would miss her when she went away on her honeymoon.

But before she was able to step close enough, Tess jumped in between them.

'Actually, I look like a *big* princess,' Tess corrected.

Lola frowned as she looked over Tess's head at her mum. She screwed up her face to show how annoying Tess was. Her mum gave her a half-smile. Lola knew that face. It was asking her to be patient. Lola took a deep breath.

The purple fabric made a lovely swishing sound around Lola's knees as she walked past Tess towards the mirror.

'Do you mind if I take a look too,

big princess?' said Lola.

Lola stood beside Tess in front of the mirror. Their reflections stared back.

'We look exactly the same!' Tess declared happily.

'So, Mum,' Lola said, lifting her hair up with her hands, 'do you think I could have an 'up' hairstyle like this?'

Tess copied her hand movements, lifting her black bob in the same way.

'Or do you think it might be better to do this?' Lola continued, holding her hair up in two pigtails. Next to her, Tess copied the second hairstyle — only one of her pigtails was very high, and the other was very low.

When Lola swung around to look at her mum, Tess swung around too. It almost felt like she had a small, colourful shadow, especially when Lola crossed her arms and the colourful shadow crossed hers. But this shadow had a very loud voice!

'Hey, look,' Tess called suddenly. 'Beau and Will are making silly window-squish faces.'

Lola turned to the shop window. Beau and Will were standing out the front of the shop. They were wearing black suits with little black bow ties. Even with their faces squished to the window pane, they still looked really cool.

Lola felt a little pang as she watched

Beau and Will crack up laughing and run away. The two of them were like best friends. Which wasn't the same thing as having a talkative shadow…

'Come on, girls,' Aunty Kay interrupted Lola's thoughts. 'It's shoe time!'

Lola had never been into such a beautiful shoe shop.

There were pink shoes with butterfly clips on the front. And red shoes that looked like they might belong to Dorothy out of *The Wizard of Oz*. There were white shoes made from shiny satin.

And, best of all, there were silver, sparkly shoes with a heel and little bows at the front.

Lola could hardly breathe as she picked them up. 'Mum?' she said, holding the shoes out. 'Pleeease?'

Lola's mum looked doubtful. 'They are lovely, Loles,' she said, 'but I think the heels are a little bit high. I'm not sure they would be very comfortable.' She gave Lola a funny look, with her head tilting towards Tess. 'You know … for *both* of you,' she added in a whisper.

'Then maybe Tess can get *these* ones,' Lola suggested, picking up a pair of silver ballet flats. They were quite similar to the ones she liked, except for the heels.

'Nuh-uh!' Tess declared. 'I want to have exactly the same shoes as Lola!'

Tess's expression reminded Lola of a storm cloud. All dark and brooding and ready to rain. 'Absolutely *exactly* the same,' she added, just to make sure everyone understood her.

'Look, sweetie,' Lola's mum said, 'I think we'll go with the ballet flats. They'll be better for *everyone*. It's a good compromise.'

Lola reluctantly put the shoes with a heel back on the shelf. If it wasn't for Tess, she was pretty sure that her mum would have let her have them.

Honestly, it's not fair, Lola thought as her mum paid for the two pairs of ballet flats.

Lola walked quickly back to the car, hoping to lose Tess for a moment. But the shadow just ran to keep up with her.

As Lola tucked herself into the tiny back seat, she turned around and saw Beau and Will laughing and chatting in the middle row.

She knew what her mum meant by the word *compromise*. Compromising was when people changed what they wanted a little bit so it would suit everyone.

Lola crossed her arms and stared out the back window, ignoring Tess's chatter.

Why am I the only one who has to compromise?

Chapter Six

The next morning, Lola got up very quietly so as not to wake Tess. She pulled on her green tracksuit pants and a grey T-shirt and went for a walk around the block.

When she got back, Rex was in the kitchen making bacon and eggs. 'Scrambled, poached or fried?' Rex asked.

'Poached, please,' Lola said.

'Me too,' came Tess's voice. 'And where did you go without me?'

Lola looked around. Tess was dressed in jeans and a shirt. Before Lola could answer, Tess had disappeared in the direction of Lola's bedroom.

'Did you have a nice walk, Loles?' Rex asked, cracking eggs into some boiling water in a saucepan.

'Yes, thanks,' she said. 'Freddie the dog barked at me. I think he wanted to come for a walk.' Freddie lived a few doors down from Lola's house. 'So I just gave him a pat through the fence,' Lola continued.

Lola was going to keep talking, but Tess interrupted.

'We're going to visit Uncle Phil today. And stay the night,' Tess said.

Lola turned around. Tess had changed. Instead of jeans and a shirt, she was now wearing tracksuit pants and a T-shirt. And a giant smile.

'See, Loles?' she said. 'We're practically *exactly* the same again. Don't we both look cool?'

Tess is copying me again!

Rex gave Lola a wink as he put a plate of poached eggs in front of her. It was as though he thought it was funny.

Lola put her head between her hands. In a way, it *was* kind of funny that Tess was trying to look like her. And she had to admit that Tess looked pretty cute.

But another part of her just felt *over* it all! The constant questions were one thing. Lola could *almost* handle that. And she was *almost* getting used to Tess following her around everywhere.

Honestly though, Tess wasn't just a shadow ... She was a real copycat.

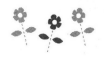

'Hey Lola, do you want to play soccer?' Will asked later that day.

Will kicked the ball from foot to foot as he spoke. Then he kicked it up to his head and butted it towards the mantelpiece.

'Yep,' Lola replied, butting it back towards him before it could do any damage.

It felt good to be walking to the park with Will. Just the two of them for once. Since Beau and Tess had arrived, she had hardly played with Will at all.

Lola wasn't sure it was very nice of her, but she had to admit she was glad that Tess and the others had gone to stay with Uncle Phil for the night.

'Now, I'll show you a trick that Beau taught me,' Will said as they arrived at the park.

Lola watched as Will kicked the ball upwards. As it rose, he leant forward. The ball rested behind his head, on the back of his shoulders. When he straightened up, he moved back very quickly, and it dropped down to his feet again.

'That is *seriously* cool!' Lola said.

'I know!' Will grinned. 'It's great hanging out with Beau. He's taught me heaps of stuff like that.'

Lola felt that strange, annoyed feeling rise through her. It wasn't something she could talk to Will about.

But the more she thought about it, the more unfair it seemed that Will got to hang out with someone his own age. Someone who could actually teach him stuff. Especially when Lola was stuck answering a gazillion questions!

'Wanna have a go?' Will asked, breaking into her thoughts.

Lola nodded. She wasn't going to let a silly feeling ruin time with Will on the soccer field.

'OK. Kick up. Now lean forward … oh *almost*, Loles!' said Will. 'Kick up, lean forward …'

Will was being really encouraging. Even when she caught the ball on her

head instead of her back, he kept on trying to teach her.

When Lola finished the trick properly for the first time, Will screamed and punched the air.

'You did it! You're a *legend,* Lola,' he said.

Lola grinned. She was happy that Rex and her mum were getting married. She was happy that Will was going to be her brother.

Even if she did have to put up with copycat Tess.

Chapter Seven

Lola put a bookmark in her book and laid it on her bedside table. She wriggled around under her doona to make her bed extra warm. Then she looked at her clock.

It was ten minutes past her normal bedtime, and her mum *still* hadn't come in for a goodnight kiss.

Finally, Lola heard her mum's footsteps down the hall.

'Hey, sweetie,' she said, coming in and sitting on Lola's bed. 'I've been trying to write some vows for the wedding ceremony. Rex has already written his, and he won't show me. It's really hard to come up with something special. Something that suits us and our family.'

Lola nodded. 'You'll think of something, Mum,' she said.

Lola's mum lifted up the doona and snuggled in next to Lola.

'And what about you, Loles? What have you been up to this afternoon?'

Lola loved this part of the day. The bit where she had her mum all to herself.

First, she told her mum about Will

teaching her the soccer trick at the park. She thrashed around under the doona, trying to demonstrate without getting out of bed.

'So, Beau taught Will the trick. And then Will taught me, and it took ages but I finally got it,' Lola explained.

Lola's mum pushed Lola's hair behind her ears. 'It's really nice, having them stay, isn't it?' she said. 'We're lucky they can look after you while Rex and I are away.'

Suddenly, Lola felt cross again. 'Why can't we come to Hawaii?' she asked. 'I don't want to stay here with Tess for a whole week.'

Before she knew it, Lola was blurting everything out. She hadn't had her mum to herself for days and it felt like there was a whole build-up of feelings that just wanted to rush out of her mouth.

'Mum, Tess copies just about *everything* I do. If I want poached eggs, she wants poached eggs. If I wear my tracksuit pants, she changes into her tracksuit pants. If I say my favourite colour is purple, she says her favourite colour is purple. And she asks more questions than … well, more questions than any other person on this planet. And she won't leave me alone. It's driving me nuts!'

'Hmm, I've noticed that Tess copies you a bit,' her mum said with a nod. 'But it's only because she admires you, Loles.

She wants to be just like you. Which, if you think about it, is kind of sweet. I guess you'll just have to be patient with her.'

'Patient?' Lola repeated. 'How come *I* have to be patient? Will doesn't have to be! He just gets to have fun with Beau.'

Lola's mum had a knowing look on her face. 'So, Will wasn't patient this afternoon when he taught you the soccer trick?' she said slowly.

Lola shrugged. She had to admit that there was at least a little bit of truth in what her mum was saying. Perhaps she *could* try to be a bit more patient with Tess.

Really, part of her enjoyed the way Tess copied her. It *was* kind of flattering.

And Tess *was* kind of cute, even with all her annoying ways.

But as her mum stroked her hair, Lola realised that there was something else making her anxious. She felt a tear trickle down her cheek. She'd never been away from her mum for a whole week before . . .

'Mum,' she whispered, 'I'm going to miss you so much when you go on your honeymoon. I wish you guys were taking me and Will.'

Lola's mum pulled her close. Her hug was tight and warm. 'Loles, I love you more than the earth and the stars. I love Will, too. And Rex loves both of you. Even when we're not with you, we are still thinking about you. We don't have to be together all the time to be … *together*,' she finished.

Lola breathed into her mum's chest. Suddenly she felt a tickle on her tummy.

'Where do you live?' her mum asked.

Lola felt a giggle brewing inside her. It wasn't just because of the tickle. It was also because she knew the game her mum was starting up. It was a game they'd played for as long as Lola could remember.

'Ryrie Court,' Lola played along.

'And where else do you live?' Lola's mum egged her on.

Lola struggled to keep her face straight. 'In my home. With my family.'

'And where else do you live?' Lola's mum asked with an extra ticklish tickle.

Lola let her answer out with a squeal and a laugh. 'In your HEART!'

Chapter Eight

Lola closed her eyes as a little puff of hairspray travelled towards her pigtails.

It was great fun to be sitting at the hairdresser's with her mum and Aunty Kay and Tess in a long row. Lola uncrossed her legs and leant closer to the mirror. Beside her, she could see Tess also uncrossing her legs, and looking in the mirror.

'What do you think of Lola's hair, Helen?' the hairdresser asked, spinning Lola's stool towards her.

'I think it's perfect,' Lola's mum said. 'I think *you're* perfect, Lola,' she added in a whisper.

'Especially with the tracksuit pants,' Lola said with a grin. Even though everyone's hair was done now, they still hadn't put on their wedding outfits. Lola couldn't *wait* for that moment.

'Mum, I can't believe we're actually, honestly, truly getting married today!' She giggled before she corrected herself, 'I mean, that *you and Rex* are getting married today.'

Lola's mum gave her a wink. She looked really pretty. Her hair was up in a loose bun, and wispy bits fell over her face. She looked back in the mirror, but she was looking at Lola, not at herself.

Suddenly, Tess scrambled up onto Lola's lap, and all Lola could see in the mirror was Tess's pigtailed head.

'Hey, Lola!' she said. 'We're allowed to wear some lip gloss!'

Back at home, Lola reached out a finger to fix up Tess's lip gloss. There seemed to be more on Tess's chin than on her lips.

Lola tapped her foot on the lounge room carpet. Her mum and Aunty Kay had been in the bedroom for *ages*.

'Loles, can you draw me a big wedding cake?' Tess asked.

Lola stared at the stack of paper on the coffee table. So far, she'd drawn a tiny cake, a medium sized cake, and a hundred flower girls, big and small.

She picked up her pencil, but just then she heard the bedroom door open.

As Aunty Kay and Lola's mum entered the lounge room, Lola's eyes grew wide. Her mouth seemed stuck in the shape of an 'O'.

Lola had always thought her mum was

pretty. But the lady in front of her was *beautiful!* The sky-blue dress had a heart-shaped neckline, with no straps. It came in at her mum's waist, and flowed down to the floor. And peeping out from under her mum's dress were a pair of dark blue shoes with diamanté buckles.

Lola let her eyes wander back up to her mum's face. Her cheeks were brushed lightly with rouge, and her eyelashes looked longer and darker than normal. With her hair up and wispy, she looked …

'Mum …' Lola breathed, 'you look, you look …'

'Like a princess. A *big* princess!' Tess finished for her.

They all cracked up laughing.

Lola almost wished the day could be frozen right here, right now.

Four girls. Laughing. In the lounge room. With a wedding ahead of them.

Lola had never been in a limousine before. For a moment, she pictured Will's reaction. He totally loved cars, and he would have loved to be travelling with Rex and Beau in a car that had been s-t-r-e-t-c-h-e-d like this.

The boys had got ready at Uncle Phil's house, so that Rex wouldn't see Lola's mum in her wedding gown. Apparently that was bad luck. But Lola knew in her heart that *nothing* could go wrong today!

The driver wore a suit with gold buttons and a cap with gold trim. When he opened the door for them, Lola couldn't help giggling.

She slid onto one of the bench seats. Tess got in next to her, and her mum and

Aunty Kay sat facing them. It felt more like a fancy room on wheels than a car.

'Are you ready, Helen?' Aunty Kay asked as the driver pulled away from the curb.

Lola noticed her mum gulp. She smoothed down her blue dress. She looked out the window and then back at Kay.

'I'm a bit nervous,' she admitted. 'You know, having to say wedding vows in front of everyone.'

'I know what a vow is,' Tess said knowingly. 'A vow is like a promise.'

Lola crossed her legs. She put her bouquet on the seat between her and Tess. Tess crossed her legs. Then she put her bouquet right on top of Lola's.

'I think there will be a *hundred* people watching us when we get out of this car, or perhaps even *fifty*,' Tess added happily.

Lola glanced at her mum. She tried to think of something to say to help her feel less nervous. But suddenly the limousine pulled to a halt.

'Ladies. We have arrived,' the driver said, tipping his cap.

Chapter Nine

It was perfect weather for a wedding in the park. The sun was shining but it wasn't too hot.

The wedding guests stood, all dressed up, in two groups with an aisle down the middle. At the end of the aisle, a white gazebo just like the one in *The Sound of Music* was decorated with flowers and bows.

Standing in the gazebo were Rex, Will and Beau. They turned and watched as the girls came down the path.

Lola thought it was funny to see Will standing so still. Normally he was jumping around and fidgeting. But now he looked very serious.

Lola and Tess walked slowly down the aisle, smiling and waving at people as they went past. Lola's mum walked behind them, holding her giant bouquet.

Lola had thought walking down the aisle might be a bit scary. But she knew heaps of the people there. She grinned as Uncle Phil blew her a kiss with both hands, and then did a funny bow. Her grandma smiled and Abbey waved to her. And she could *feel* everyone's happiness. It wasn't scary at all. It was fun!

When they got to the gazebo, Lola stood between her mum and Tess. Lola's mum and Rex held hands.

'Ladies and gentlemen,' said the wedding celebrant who stood in front of them on a little platform. 'We are gathered here today to celebrate the union of Rex and Helen.'

Lola glanced around. The guests were standing all around the gazebo now, in a semi-circle. Lola twirled her bouquet until it was time for Rex to say his vows.

'I promise,' he began. Lola noticed

that Rex had to clear his throat and start again.

'I promise to love and honour the beautiful Helen. I promise to respect her.' He looked at Lola before he continued. 'And to care for the lovely daughter I've always wanted ...'

Lola felt her cheeks redden, but it was a nice kind of embarrassment.

'Hey, what about me?' Will interrupted from next to Rex.

The guests all laughed. Rex smiled. 'And you too, if you behave,' he added.

It took a while for the laughter to die down. Lola smiled but she couldn't quite relax. Part of her was worried for her mum.

Lola hoped that she had been able to think up some wedding vows of her own.

Lola gulped as her beautiful mum opened her mouth and closed it again. Then Rex cupped his hands around her mum's, and this seemed to help.

'I promise to love and honour Rex,' Lola's mum said slowly and clearly. The guests were completely silent. 'I promise to cherish our beautiful family.

'And I promise that each of you will be right with me, always, even when we're not together.' Lola's mum looked across at Will. Then at Rex. Then her eyes landed on Lola and stayed there.

Lola pushed her lips together so she wouldn't cry. She knew what her mum was going to say next.

'Because you all live right here,' Helen said, clutching the bouquet against her chest, 'in my heart.'

Chapter Ten

Lola sat at the kids' table at the wedding reception. Her feet bumped against her empty rose-petal basket. It had been fun throwing the petals over her mum and Rex. She and Tess had giggled all the way through the photo session too. When the photographer had told them to say 'cheese', Lola knew that was supposed to help them smile. But they hadn't needed any help at all. Lola's face ached from all the smiles. Real smiles.

'Hey Lola, let's go and get thirds,' Tess said, popping the last piece of wedding cake on her plate into her mouth.

Lola groaned and shook her head. 'I think I'm full, Tess,' she said.

'But you can *never* be full of chocolate cake with pink icing!' Tess protested. 'All right then, let's just get more punch,' she added, giving Lola a little punch on the arm.

Lola smiled and followed Tess to the drinks' table. She looked around the reception centre. Some of the guests had swapped tables to chat with other friends. Others stood around, clinking glasses, chatting and laughing.

Lola looked at the band, which was warming up on the stage at the front of the room. Then she used the ladle to serve herself and Tess glasses of punch.

As the girls walked back to their table, the band started playing.

Lola watched as Rex took her mum's hand and they walked to the dance floor.

Lola knew that the dance they were doing was called a 'waltz'. She loved the way her mum's dress swished around as she moved. She loved the way Rex held her around the waist and dipped her down.

She watched as he lifted her mum back to standing position.

Soon, heaps of the guests had joined them. Lola giggled as she spotted Will twirling on the dance floor with Aunty Kay and raising his eyebrows again.

'Lola?' Tess said, tugging at her arm. 'Lola?'

Lola looked back at Tess. Tess had a worried expression as she pushed her chair back from the table and glanced down at her feet.

'I'm sorry about the shoes,' she said. 'I'm sorry I made you get the same ones as me. I know you really wanted the other ones. I hope you like them, just a little bit?'

Lola gave Tess a special smile. She put her feet next to Tess's in a line. 'I *love* the shoes, Tess,' she said. 'And I reckon they're *dancing* shoes! Should we try them?'

Lola loved how Tess's face lit up. Her grin ran from ear to ear.

As they walked towards the dance floor, Tess grabbed Lola's hand. She pulled Lola down towards her so she could whisper in her ear. 'You are the bestest cousin in the whole, entire universe,' she said to Lola. 'You're a *legend.*'

Lola squeezed Tess's hand. She thought about how Will had taught her the soccer trick, and then told her she was a legend. Maybe Will found *her* annoying sometimes.

But then again, maybe that was all part of being family.

As she pulled Tess onto the dance floor, Lola leant down and whispered in her ear. '*You're* the bestest too, Tess,' she said. '*You* are a legend.'

Lola blinked sleepily and looked up at her bedside table. Her rose-petal basket was no longer empty — it was now full of tiny chocolates that she and Tess had collected from all the tables after they'd exhausted themselves dancing.

At the end of the wedding she had fallen

asleep on two chairs pushed together. Tess and Will and Beau had done the same on some chairs opposite.

Lola had woken up when Rex carried her to the car, but she'd pretended she was still asleep.

Later that night, Lola woke up for a moment and was glad to hear Tess's breathing on the trundle bed next to her.

Lola knew she would be in her mum's heart while her mum was in Hawaii. She hoped her mum and Rex would have the best time ever.

Because Lola knew she was going to have a great time, right here, at home. Even if she *did* miss her mum and Rex, it was pretty amazing that she had Will and Beau and Aunty Kay, and even Tess, to look after her.

And they were family too.

Collect them all!

go girl
Brilliant Besties

♥Chrissie Perry ♥ Rowan McAuley
♥Meredith Badger

go girl
School Spirit

Meredith Badger ● Rowan McAuley

go girl
Super Sporty

Chrissie Perry ● Thalia Kalkipsakis